W9-BJM-192

HOLLER, CHILD

Also by LaToya Watkins

Perish

HOLLER, CHILD

stories

LATOYA WATKINS

An imprint of Penguin Random House LLC
penguinrandomhouse.com

"The Mother" originally published in *Ruminate*. "Cutting Horse" originally published in *McSweeney's Quarterly Concern*. "Tipping" originally published in *A Public Space*. "Moving the Animal" originally published in *The Sun* as "Took Us All Like We Was His." "Vigil" originally published in *West Branch*. "Sweat" originally published in *The Kenyon Review*.

LIBRARY OF CONGRESS CATALOGING-IN-PUBLICATION DATA

Names: Watkins, LaToya, author.
Title: Holler, child: stories / LaToya Watkins.
Other titles: Holler, child (Compilation)
Description: New York: Tiny Reparations Books, an imprint of Penguin Random House LLC, [2023]
Identifiers: LCCN 2023002430 (print) | LCCN 2023002431 (ebook) | ISBN 9780593185940 (hardcover) | ISBN 9780593185964 (ebook)
Subjects: LCGFT: Short stories.
Classification: LCC PS3623.A869445 H65 2023 (print) | LCC PS3623.A869445 (ebook) | DDC 813/.6—dc23/eng/20230502
LC record available at https://lccn.loc.gov/2023002430
LC ebook record available at https://lccn.loc.gov/2023002431

Printed in the United States of America
1st Printing

For Mom, Wal, and Shay: a tree and her first fruits.
Let us always remember ourselves.

CONTENTS

HOLLER, CHILD

THE MOTHER

....

For the Only Son

The visits done died down a little bit now. When it first happened, a week ago, all kind of reporters was camped out in my yard. Some still come. The rustlers, like this one sitting in front of me. They still asking bout Hawk. Bout how he come to call hisself the Messiah. Bout who his daddy is, but I ain't got nothing for them.

I look out the window I keep my chair pulled up next to. Ain't no sun, just cold and still. Banjo lift his head up when he see my eyes on him, but it don't take him long to let it fall back on his paws. He done got his rope a little tangled up. Can't move too much with it like that, but he can breathe and lay down. He all right. I'll go out and work out the knot when I can—when this gal leave.

It's cold out there, but I ain't too worried bout Banjo. He got natural insulation. I'm the one cold and I'm on the inside—supposed to be on the inside, cause I'm a person. I ain't got no insulation, though. This old house ain't got none neither. The window is rickety and wood-framed. Whole house is. Whole house ain't no thicker—no stronger than a big old piece of plywood. Ain't nothing to separate me from the cold wind outside but the glass and the pane.

This gal sitting there shivering like white folk ain't used to the cold. Everybody—even me—know white folks is makers of the cold. And this one here white as the snow on the ground out there. Ain't no whole lot of snow; not enough to stick, to keep these wandering folks like her out my face. I wonder if the snow reached Abilene fore Hawk and his white folks left life for good. Fore he crucified hisself and took all them other people with him. Wonder if he left this world clean.

"Trees outside my window naked all the time," I say, and I pretend in my mind I was raised here and not on Thirty-Fourth. Just pretend I been on the East Side all along. On the East Side, where good-time whoring didn't never catch, even if being strung out on drugs did. Where snow come to cover up the dirt in places where grass don't never grow like icing covering up chocolate cake or brownies or anything dark and sweet. The East Side. Where you be happy poor and don't try to pretend you can fuck your way out. I just pretend in my mind I was brought up poor and wasn't never no whore.

"Ma'am?" the girl say, like I done confused her. Lines come up on her forehead. Make all them big freckles look like they shifting. Like she got skin like a sow. Skin that got a life of its own and move and breathe and filthy. She run her hand through her stringy red hair. White-folk hair. I pray to Jesus she don't leave none of it in my carpet.

"Some folks see green in the summer. But come this time of year, everybody trees look like them out yonder." I nod my head at the window. I want to make sure she get a good look at the naked, flimsy trees out there. "Like they naked. Like they poor," I say after a while.

"Oh. Yes," she say, nodding her head and letting her eyes open real wide like she recognize something I just said. She lift up her head a little bit to look past me—to look out my window. "But won't you let the dog in? He's so small for the cold." I don't say nothing, but she say something else. "Joshua's father, Ms. Hawkins. I asked about him. Remember?"

I sigh real loud. I want her to know that what she asking me to talk bout don't come easy. I'd rather tell her my momma was a junkie whore just like her momma, and the little two-room shanty the government help me rent now would've been a mansion in the sky for either one of them. I want to tell her I was fourteen and pregnant when Butch Ugewe come to the Hitching Post and saved me. Made me his. A honest woman. I want to finally tell somebody—anybody—how Momma ain't put up no fight. How all Butch had to do was offer her a little bit of under-the-table money and she let him take me. But I can't.

I shrug my shoulders. "Everything different when you traveling through places," I say, thinking bout where I growed up and how pretty everything looked on the outside. How the womens that lived in Ms. Beaseley's whorehouse on Thirty-Fourth was poor and throwed out by the world, but couldn't nobody tell it by looking at them on the outside. Men couldn't even see the ruin of the place they was in once they got past Ms. Beaseley's nice lawn and long country porch. The painted up women with twice-douched snatches covered up all the ugly they was pushing theyselfs into.

I move my eyes away from the window and put them on the girl. She got a long bird face and her teeth stick out a little too far for her tiny mouth. I can tell by the way the sides of her mouth drooping down, she ain't used to being in a place like mine. I don't want to make her feel more uncomfortable, so I don't say nothing bout the pregnant-looking roach crawling slow up the wood-paneled wall behind her head.

"I reckon peoples be just like them trees, you see?" Her face blank. I can tell she don't see. "Everybody got a season to go through being ugly and naked." I laugh a little bit.

"Yes, ma'am," she say. Then she sigh and let her eyes roll halfway round in the sockets. "We all have problems, but can we—"

"That enough heat on you?" I ask. "Can't never keep this old lean-to warm. That enough heat on you—" I stop myself from calling her "miss." I want to spank the back of my own hand. She younger than me. Probably by bout twenty years or more. Still, I want to make sure the old electric heater sitting on the cracked and splintered floor, humming near her feet, is doing what it's supposed to do. Sometimes it blow cold air instead of heat. I want to make sure it ain't freezing her.

She look confused bout my question. Them lines in her head get deeper and she start shaking her foot a little. She want her story for the paper. Want to find out if I think my son was God like them folks that was following behind him in Abilene.

Last time I saw him, Hawk told me he was the *real* son of God, and Jesus was a scud. Told me he was the truth, and me and the rest of the world best believe it. Dust storm was swirling outside like it was the end of things that day. He walked into my life after more than twenty years, and all I could wonder was how he found me. Walked in and spread his arms like a giant black bird and said, "Woman, you are the mother of *I Am*."

I shake my head. "Hawk was always a good boy. Always. After Butch died, he helped me raise hisself for as long as he could. He did everything he could to make sure we was tooken care of. Hawk wasn't but nine, but he sure learned to do what he had to do."

Hawk asked me bout his daddy when he was still a little boy. I told him it was Butch, and Butch denied it right in his face. Later on, after Butch was dead and my legs was back to welcoming mens all night long, I told him bout Mary and Jesus and me and hisself. Tucked him into bed and he looked up at me like I was something. Everything was still in the house that night. No tricks, no Butch, no drugs. And I wanted him to be still and special and good, so I told him the same story I heard as a girl. Same story the preacher shouted over the pulpit some Sundays when Ms. Beaseley would drag every whore in the house down to Good Shepherd's Baptist Church. Cept I made him the star. *Truth is you dropped right out the sun to my arms*, I told him. *I was just a girl. Ain't know nothing bout mens and babies. You special, Hawk. You special. God your daddy. You special.* I wanted him to be normal. I ain't want him to be no whore son. Folks would've judged him for what I was.

When Hawk first died, the papers and stuff ain't bother with me too much. Reckon wasn't really no way for them to know who I was. I hadn't been his momma since I gave him up. But after his body went missing from the morgue last week, all kind of stuff done printed in the paper. Newspapers coming to get my story—to know bout Hawk and me and how everything happened. Some of them say I can make money and be rich, but I want to be where I am. I want to be happy poor. I tried most of my life to fuck myself rich. I don't want to pretend. I'm gone be where I'm at.

Fore his body went missing, it was all scandal. It was a story printed in the paper bout him messing with a little girl up there in Abilene. Say he was charged with aggravated sexual assault on a child cause he used some kind of doctor instrument to see if the little girl had some kind of cancer in her woman part. Paper say he was doctoring them Abilene folks and ain't have the right training. Had his own community—own world out there. He was God and made soap and growed food, and them folks gave him everything they had so he could have more than they did. Hawk got thirty years in prison that I ain't never know bout for doctoring on that little girl. Least that's what thc paper say. Called it some kind of rape or something. Say he made all them folks kill theyselves so he wouldn't have to do his time.

Now, though, since they can't figure out what done happened to his body, they printing stuff bout proving who he really was, eyewitness accounts of his miracles, and the search for his real daddy. I can't tell them nothing. I don't know what to think. All I know is I don't talk to the big ones. I only let them small-timers come through my door. They don't come promising nothing. They just want to hear me.

The lady look at the pad she been writing on. "Yes, but Butch Ugewe wasn't his biological father, right?"

I try to dig back to stuff I remember from church and Ms. Beaseley talking. She was like some kind a madame preacher. Always saying the world need whores so the good Lord can have folks to save.

I finally smack my lips and say, "Shoot. Baby, you gone have to forgive me. *Bonanza* bout to happen." I get up slow cause my body don't move the way it used to. I cross over her legs and say scuse me, making my way to the TV. I push the button on the thing and it make a loud popping noise that make the girl jump a little bit. "Ain't no need to be afraid, chile," I say, making my way back over her legs. "Things old round here. We all got our tics."

She sigh. "Yes, but Butch Ugewe—"

"You a God-fearing woman, umm . . . What's your name again, baby?" I ask and wait for her to tell me for the third time.

She look at me like she don't know what to say. Then she say, "Rhoda. Rhoda Pearson, and I was raised Catholic." She kind of tilt her head up a little, like Catholic is better than regular God-fearing.

"Oh," I say, and I don't know what else to say cause I don't know much bout them Catholics. "Y'all go by the Bible?"

She nod her head and shrug her shoulders at the same time. Her lips is straight across like a line drawed on a stick-figure face. Like she don't know what that got to do with anything—her religion.

I think bout my last conversation with Hawk. He talked bout earthly fathers and his heavenly one. "Well, you know in one them books, Matthew, I think, when everybody get to begetting somebody else?" She nod her head. "Well, Hawk told me that ain't had nothing to do with Jesus momma. That's all bout Joseph. The stepdaddy."

"That's right. The genealogy in that book *is* Joseph's," she say, nodding her head. She interested in what I got to say now.

"Well, if that Jesus, the one you and half the world *think* was the Messiah, and his disciples ain't care nothing about who was and wasn't his real daddy, why we always trying to prove DNA and mess today?"

She laugh a little and then sigh. She sit the pad down on her lap and look at the old TV I got sitting on top the big floor model. *Bonanza* going and she act like she into it.

This one chubby. She got brown hair and I know it's shedding soon as she walk in. Got strings of it all over her shirt, and it don't look healthy at all. She holding her little notepad close to her chest like it got secrets about the world in it. When she sit down on the couch, the plastic I keep it covered with sound like it's screaming. She look around the room until she land her eyes on me. Look like she trying to place the dates on my old-time furniture.

"It ain't antique," I say. "Just old. Stuff ain't nobody else want no more."

She smile and nod her head. I sit down in my rocking chair next to the window.

"I hated to hear about your son's death, Ms. Hawkins," she say. I wave her words away with my hand. She keep going. "I hate for any mother to lose her child. I'm a mother myself, Ms. Hawkins," she say, grabbing at her breast with her chubby hand. "Miscarried four times before my son was born. I know what it's like to lose a child." Her eyes look sad like she want me to be sad with her. She looking at me hard. I wave my hand at her again.

"I hadn't seen a hair on Hawk head in years fore I saw them surrounding his place on the news. I loved him. Mommas always love they boys. But Hawk been gone from me longer than two weeks."

"I take it you all weren't close," she say, looking at me from the corners of her eyes like she done found out something important or I done gave the best gossip of the day.

And I think on it for a minute. The last time I saw him, I cooked for him. Smothered pork chops, collards, sweet potatoes, and hot water cornbread. It was the first time I had cooked for him since fore drugs took hold of me. Fore I lost him—fore they took him. He wouldn't eat the pork chops. Said they don't do that at the House of Joshua. Said they don't do a lot of other things. They don't bathe with regular bath soap. They make theirs out of lye. Said pork chops and real soap is grounds for excommunication.

He brought a white man to my house that day. Short, stocky something. His skin was bout as pale as the off-white paint on my wall and he was bald at the top but had his hair swooped over like he wanted to hide it. I wanted to tell him his head was slick as a table even with that hair swooped over, but I had seen too many white, bald, swooped heads to let my tongue go like that. He didn't never open his wide rubber lips—not the whole time he was here. Just stood there like some kind of little person bodyguard.

Hawk told me I looked good. Said he could see clean in my spirit, and I ain't apologize to him bout leaving him to be with myself. For never coming to get him when them white folks took him from me. I ain't tell him I was sorry for letting him go out into the world eleven years old and full of my lies. I ain't apologize bout nothing.

Apologize for what? Hawk ain't end up so bad. Turned out better than he would've if I wouldn't have messed up. Foster family what got him, kept him. Made him go to school. Made him stick with it. He went to school for theology. Found hisself in there, he said. Sat at my table and tossed words I ain't understand around, like a empty grocery bag blowing in a dust storm. Seeing him that day with his fun-sized driver and bodyguard and being served by them white folks like he was sweet Jesus hisself made me feel good bout saving him from being a whore son.

Sat at my table and told me he found his daddy. I wanted to find out who he found. Wanted to know who his daddy was myself. All his life I had tried to look for signs in his body. Something to tell me which one of them mens had made me have him. Looked at his height. Even that day, his tall body swayed when he walked through my front door. He had to bend—kind of fold hisself just to get through. His eyes was like two light chestnuts, but his skin was dark as pure brass. He was a big, muscular man. Look like he could crush you without trying.

Hawk stretched out his hands like he was bout to be pent up on a cross and asked me in his thunder voice, *Woman, would thou like to be saved? Set free?* Then he told me his story bout being my savior—savior to all mens and womens. Savior of the world. Told me he had a place for me in paradise. Told me he wanted me to come to Abilene.

"We was close enough," I finally say to Chubby. She write on her pad.

"What was he like as a boy, Ms. Hawkins?" she ask, smiling. I see some green stuff in her teeth and it make me smile too. I don't say nothing bout it. Just sit there smiling back at her.

I shrug my shoulders. "Hawk was taken from me early on, but

all his time with me, them first eleven years, he was a regular boy. Wanted what regular little boys want. Went where regular little boys went—"

"I know, I know, but he had to be different in some kind of way, Ms. Hawkins. There must have been something significant about him. He led all of those people in Abilene. Most of them followed him for more than twenty years, and a lot of people say they saw him perform miracles. People died for him, Ms. Hawkins," she say, holding her hands out in front of herself, letting them shake a little like she having a fit. She finally drop them back down to her lap and sigh.

"Was he anything like his father, ma'am?" she ask.

I look at her long and hard. She just a little younger than me. Look like she probably in her forties or something. Got a round pie face like a trick used to come see me when I was still a little girl. He didn't never seem to mind my young naked bottom on the nasty bare mattress. I always imagined him going back home to nice clean sheets. Leaving me dirty and ruined and spilling over with his seeds. Now I imagine him as her daddy.

I let myself smile. "You from here, young lady?" I ask. And she look like she don't want to answer, but she do.

She nod her head and smile. "Been away most of my adult life, though. Never wanted to write for the *Avalanche*. Too small. Everything about this place is small," she say, looking around my den. "Alas, I am here. The winding roads of life, huh?"

Her eyes land on the only picture hanging on the wall. The eight-by-ten frame is crooked and dusty. I haven't touched it in years. She got questions in her eyes. The black woman in the picture smiling with her hand halfway covering her mouth, and a white man touching—look like a soft touch—the side of her face and looking at her with love in his eyes. A dark image in the background blurred out of focus, but it look like a child playing or something. "May I?" she ask, pointing at the picture, standing up like she gone walk toward it.

"Gone," I say. "If it tickle your fancy." I turn my head and look out the window. Banjo resting on his paws, tied up to the tree. I think about maybe putting a blanket out there so he won't have to lay on top of the snow. He old and tired and ain't barked to complain bout being tied up. Tied up to that tree is all Banjo know, though.

"Oh, it's the photo that came with the frame," she say out loud, and then she laugh a little bit and start making her way back to the couch. "So is he? Is—or *was*—your son anything like his father?"

"You anything like *your* father?" I ask. Her eyes get wide and she look down at her hand.

"I suppose I used to be. He's nothing like himself these days. Alzheimer's. He . . ." She trail off and sniff. "He dies some every day." She look sad and I feel kind of sorry bout pushing her, but I know her kind. She want her story. She'll cry to get it.

"Guess we all got a little bit of our daddies in us. If we dig deep enough, we find that. Hawk ain't no different. He was his father's son."

"Who was his father, Ms. Hawkins? If you don't mind my asking." She add the last part on kind of quick.

I shake my head cause now I can't get the picture of my old

trick out of my head. I see him on top of me, with Alzheimer's. He drooling on my face and calling me a strange name.

"I was Hawk daddy after Butch was gone. After I was gone, he had a foster daddy. I'm sure he had pieces of all us in him," I say.

"Yeah, but I meant . . ." she say and just stop talking. She tilt her head to the side and smile. "Yeah."

Hawk told me that Jesus was a scud and his disciples was tricked. Told me I couldn't get to heaven if I didn't go through him. Called hisself the "Great Mediator." Called God El Shaddai; said El Shaddai told him I was pure as a virgin, so he choosed me. Said that white man, who name was Troy, was the one true disciple of the one true Messiah. I laughed at him and that white man that day.

Woman, my family are those who do the will of my father, he said that day, looking at me all serious. *All real men, like this one*, he said, pointing at Troy. *Woman, these men have cast their homes, their businesses, and their people aside. Everything to follow the one true Messiah.* He was nodding his head and poking his lips out like he used to do when he was young—when he in trouble and wanted to cry his way out.

I asked, *You mean for me to believe you Jesus hisself, Hawk?*

He just shook his head. *I mean for you to believe I am Joshua the Messiah. Jesus was a scud. We—my Father and I—we chose you from the beginning. I mean—we mean*, he said, pointing to Troy and up toward the ceiling, *for you to believe the truth. To carry it. To live it.*

. . .

This one is a homely-looking thing. Look like a baby—a mutt baby. She mixed. Black and white, I think. She ain't got no pen and pad, but she done brought a official-looking white woman with her. Woman look like she FBI or something. Got a real straight face and a long thick body. Something like a giant or a angel or something out of this world. Coal-black hair pulled back in a bun. It look wet. I want to thank her for at least tying it up fore coming here. But her face—the way the bones in her cheeks all high and tight—make it look like she can't smile if she want to, like she evil and mean, and I don't want to say nothing to her. She ain't the one here for the story, though. I can tell by her empty eyes. It's the young'un—the mutt want the story.

She look bout fifteen—a tall fifteen. Look like white trash with drops of black up in her. Hair that dirty blond a lot of mutts born with, and it's long and stringy and thin for her kind. She don't look right with the FBI lady. Make me think bout Hawk and the last time he was here with his tiny bodyguard. They looked lopsided just like these two. Cept with them it was they builds. These two gals is lopsided in other ways. They lopsided in what they got. One get to be all white and one don't. Anybody can look at them and see that.

The young'un look like she belong here—here on the East Side with the poor black folks. Look like one of us, so out of all the wonderers that been in here asking bout my boy, I offer her a cup of water. I don't want to offer her FBI agent nothing, but I gone head and do it. The young'un say yes, but, just like I knew she would, FBI say no. She looking around like she expecting to see a roach or something, and I kind of want to tell her that they usually don't go to crawling till ain't nobody looking for them or when I turn the lights off for bed. I want to tell her they like bedbugs, cept they don't want my blood. They want the crumbs I drop that been dropped down to me.

She look at the young'un and nod her head toward me, and the young'un open her mouth and say, "We aren't really supposed to be here. Ms. Gertrude risked her fostering to bring me."

FBI—Gertrude—reach out her hand and let it slide from the top of the girl head all the way down to her shoulders, and I hope she don't leave no hair on my couch. "It is really not a problem, Chloe," she say, and I realize she ain't no original American. Sound like she from somewhere hard and cold like Germany or Russia. I had a trick that had been to both places and his body always felt like ice pops. He was hard and rough and I couldn't never do nothing good for him. "You have been through so much already. I only want to help." Then she do something that surprise me. She spread her lips and smile like it hurt.

The young'un smile back at her fore she look back at me. "I need you to tell about Joshua Hawkins. They printed your name in the paper, and Ms. Gertrude—she's my foster mother since everything happened—"

"Maybe you should tell her what happened, child," Gertrude say.

The girl ignore her and say, "I'm Chloe Hawkins, ma'am. Joshua was my father." She say her words with a straight face, like I'm posed to know. Like I been expecting her or something. But Hawk ain't say nothing bout no kids when he come here three years ago. Ain't say nothing bout no wife either. Matter of fact, Hawk ain't really say nothing bout hisself as a person. He only talked bout hisself as God. I look at her skin and know she carrying somebody blackness. She tall like Hawk and her eyes sit big in her head like his.

"Oh," is all I can say. I don't feel nothing like I think a grandmother would. I don't feel nothing like wrapping her up and warming her from the world. I want to, though. Want to feel how I forgot to feel with Hawk. Want to want to go bake a tray of cookies or a pie or something like that. But I don't. Just sit here and wait for her mouth to guide me.

"I had twelve brothers and sisters," she say, letting her eyes drop to her lap. "They're all gone now. Died with my father and mothers. I was with Gertrude. They placed me there after . . ." Her words just stop.

She look down at her hands and start bending her fingers back like she want to pop them or something. She look back up and her eyes shining different cause they got tears in them. She sniff and sigh, and I know.

"You her, ain't you?" I ask, looking in her eyes. They chestnuts like Hawk's. They just like his. His eyes was the first thing I noticed when I slid him out my snatch like shit. They was brown and nutty and I knowed nothing that beautiful didn't come from me. I wanted to pop them out and save them—hold them close to my heart. I loved his eyes. They was always his very best thing. They was always the thing I wanted to save from seeing the whore in me.

"You the one he got in trouble bout touching," I say. "You my grandbaby?" I ask.

She nod her head and sniff hard. The water in her eyes start to spill on out, and Gertrude rub her back. "I know he wasn't certified or anything, but he would never hurt me. Not the way they say. He was a good doctor. All he ever—"

"It is okay, Chloe," Gertrude say, spitting a little on the last letter of each word she say. "Remember what the doctor says. Do not make excuses for him. The only way to face it—"

"Stop it, Ms. Gertrude," she say loud enough to cause the lady's eyes to get wide but still soft enough to not be disrespectful. "Just stop it."

Gertrude nod her head and look at me. Chloe look at me too. "They took me from home after the whole thing got out. After the mole leaked it. They took me and now I don't have a home anymore."

"Yes, you do, Chloe. You are with Gertrude," Gertrude say real fast and sloppy like she got to hurry and get it out. Like if she don't hurry up Chloe won't understand that she want to be there for her.

"I know," Chloe say real soft. "But I want my family. I want them to rest in peace and not lies," she say, the words spilling out her mouth like fire ants from a stepped-on nest. "I want to follow the truth. I believe my father was him—the Messiah. He lives. I don't care what people say. How they want him to look. He—"

"Okay, Chloe. Okay," Gertrude say, nodding her head.

Chloe smile and rest her back in my couch. She trying to get comfortable and I want to tell her that the springs poking out ain't gone let her. I want to tell her that I had that old couch since Hawk was a little boy. I done fucked and come on that couch. I done shot up and throwed up on that couch, but I don't say nothing. I let her try to find her place in it.

"Please, ma'am," she say without looking at me. She looking at her hands in her lap. "My father was the son of El Shaddai. I know that. But there have to be witnesses in the world. I'm a witness. But you have to tell them—tell them who his father was," she say, looking up at me. Her eyes filling up like a glass under the faucet. "Tell all these folks so they can finally know. Tell them so they can be saved too."

I think bout Hawk and El Shaddai and God and this little half-something gal sitting in front of me. She want the story—acting like she need it. And Hawk was a good boy, and his story was really the only thing he ever asked me for. Wanted his daddy. Wanted to know the truth bout hisself, and I ain't had no way of knowing myself. He went on out and made his own truth, and I ain't got half a right to take that away from him.

All them skinned knees and unfixed lunches and bullies and growling stomachs and me high or on my back or not there flash fore my eyes. And his last visit do too. The one where he brought the white man with him. How he left with tears in his eyes cause I laughed when he asked me to come follow him in Abilene. How his lips quivered like they did when he was six months old and bout to cry. How he was asking me to be the momma of God cause I had told him when he was little I was. How I struck a match to my cigarette and laughed in his face. I see it all, and I know Hawk wasn't never confused. He knowed I was a junkie whore and ain't know who his daddy was, but he wanted me to be something else. He wanted me to be what I said I was.

He went out and made me the momma of God. I laugh a little, thinking bout people following an old junkie whore, bowing to her like she pure and righteous and clean. Like she the momma of God. I look in Chloe lonely, lied-to eyes, and I wonder if Hawk would've done that exam on her if I told him his momma was a whore when he was little. Wonder if he would've been a messiah if he seen the truth back then. Wonder what would've happened if I'd have popped out his eyes after he slid into the world.

I open my mouth, thinking bout what Hawk made me. What I want him to be.

"Baby, I ain't knowed no man when Hawk was made. Matter of fact, I called him Hawk cause it seem to me he flew right out the sky into my arms," I say. "And if you want me to, I'll tell the world."

And that little girl smile so wide it feel like the sun shining on me for the first time ever.

CUTTING HORSE

This horse being in my backyard got me in some kind of trouble. That much I know. Since I got home from work, I been sitting back here flipping between news channels, watching this woman, her dude, and the laws on the national stations and folks looking for this horse on the local ones.

It was seven horses got out the gates of them stables around the corner, but she the only one still ain't back with them. Now, they saying she been stolen. Say they received reports that the suspect, a black male, holding the horse in the area. The police chief told the cameras they got to proceed with caution cause they don't want the horse life in no more danger than it already is.

And I'm thinking, *Who put horse stables in the middle of the suburbs anyway?* When me and my cousin Moochie stacked our paper long enough to buy our land, we went out past Lubbock city limits, out there by the hogpens, and built our stables and shit there. You do that to give the horses room to roam, to feel wild, to feel kind of free. Ain't no room for all them horses on that little patch of land around the corner. All it is is a little corner. Not even two acres. Our horses never ran, closed gate or open. Forty acres of land was enough for them to feel free.

Them sirens, the way they going off, don't make me move from my love seat, from my special place under the tarp tent I set up last spring. My tarp tent ain't nothing real neat or grand. It's more like a sloppy fort that I done set up in the middle of the yard. Got four sturdy wooden beams from the hardware store and just draped the blue tarp over them, nailing it to the top corners and letting the rest hang down like a pharaoh hat. Like I said, it ain't nothing grand, but I like it and it's mine.

Instead of getting up and running, trying to get where somebody need me to be, do what somebody need me to do, I take a drag of the blunt I rolled earlier and keep my eyes focused on the TV screen. This weed make me cough, though. It's some good shit. Them boys on Parker Circle always got good shit.

Through all that, the sirens and the coughing, I keep my eyes on the woman on the TV screen I got sitting on the stand right in front of me. She yelling at the police that's hovering over her. She mad about how they done slammed her and her dude down on the cement; she got her arms spread out, her hands flat against the ground, and her mouth going. Her dude got the side of his face to the ground and his hands already bound behind his back. He quiet. Mouth closed. Almost like he dead, but ain't nobody been shot yet.

"See! You see my hands? They on the ground! Don't shoot!" she saying to the police officer that just cuffed her dude's hands.

"We unarmed, y'all!" she say to whoever videoing the whole thing. "We ain't done nothing! They messing with us for nothing!"

The camera zoom in close to her man face. His eyes look empty. Look shook, like while all these scared men drawed on him, he scared too, like he remembering what happed to Michael and Eric and Alton and Philando and all of them. I'm remembering them too. Looking at him all scared, I'm remembering them too.

I turn my eyes to the blunt, mostly cause I know what happen next. Hold it out in front of me and look at it like I can't believe I got it in my hands. I'm looking at it like I ain't roll it myself, like I ain't never seen one. "Damn," I say. "This some good shit." And I mean it.

I work hard loading them packages part-time for the parcel company every morning, and this here—this blunt be the best part of my day. The part I work to get to all morning long. This the part where I connect with me, with who I used to be. Every day, I can't believe I survived and made it to this part.

I hear the sound of gunshots firing from the TV, but I don't turn my head back to it. I don't want to see it. It's the real reason I turned my eyes to this blunt. I done watched this ten times today and I don't want to watch it again, especially when I think about them sirens out on the street. How they looking for me.

Instead of looking at the screen, I look out to the corner of the yard at the horse, and think about how a hour ago this beautiful beast just pranced up to the orange tarp I put up on the side of the fence I tore down. She a liver chestnut color, and her coat shine like rusty pennies. That shine, that mane, all of it remind me of home.

I think about my cowboy hats and how people used to laugh cause I was part gangster, part cowboy. How I loved breeding horses but I needed the game to do it. I think about what I gave up to be here. And I wonder what all this mean. Why this horse brought all her trouble to me.

A hour ago, I sat on my love seat, tugged at a blunt with my teeth, and spat paper speckles on the ground. I heard my wife car start up from the other side of the fence, the side that's closed in, and I kind of froze. Sat there holding the blunt between both my index fingers and thumbs, like a taco, until I heard her car back out and drive off.

Cole, my wife, ain't come outside to tell me she was leaving. In fact, she ain't come and look for me after she made it in from work a few hours earlier at all, but that's a normal thing these days. She mad with me and I'm tired of her. She want to finish undoing me so I'll be like she want me to be, but I won't let her. I quit peeling parts of myself off after I realized I was the only one doing the peeling. She was keeping herself. Everybody around us keeping theyself. I'm the only one can't be me.

I don't know where she left to. She try to make her storming out mysterious most days. She might've gone blazing toward the baby daycare to pick him up before it close or to the grocery store to get something to cook tonight.

I know her lips was poked out and steam was flowing from her ears. And I know she probably called her momma to complain that she sick of me. That she should've married up, not down. That I ain't never gone be the man she want me to be.

When I was sure she was gone, I licked the edges of the blunt and curled it tight into itself. Then I picked up the lighter from the lawn table I pulled under the tent last spring, and I held the blunt under the lighter until it was dry. That's when I smiled. Right after that, the horse pranced up.

This horse that done made her way to my yard got a shiny coat. Somebody take good care of her, but that don't mean she don't know she captive. She been working on that same patch of grass since I opened the gate and let her back here. She ain't no gypsy horse like the ones I loved breeding. Them still the most beautiful beasts to me. All that mane look like ponytails all over they bodies. And we kept ours looking fresh, like they was for shows or something. We pay the hood beautician, Lulu Shepherd, good money to come out and style and condition they mane every week and we fed them like kings. But they wasn't no real show horses. We couldn't be part of that world. We just rode them and showed them off in our hood. Riding the kids, Juneteenth parades, and birthday parties on the East Side. They made our folks happy. Feel like somebodies sometimes. The illegitimacy of our business might've kept us out of the show world, but it didn't keep them Good Old Boys from buying my gypsies. My horses was everything.

This one look like a quarter. Them some nice horses too. News folks say all seven of them cutting horses. I wonder if these city news reporters even know cutting about more than competitions and stuff. I wonder if the owners even know how important cutting was out on the open range. Folks around here think cutting all about sport, but that ain't where it started.

Cutting horse born to judge, to discern, and most folks, like them around the corner, got them sitting under some panel being judged. Cutting horse know which cattle need branding or sick or any other thing a cow can't open his mouth and say. Know how to read other beasts and move they minds, master them. My granddaddy used to say you make your horse your friend, not your servant. That way they want to do stuff for you. Horse don't want no master cause they masters all on they own. Specially cutters. Them folks, the ones looking for the horse and the ones reporting it stole, don't know how much this here horse know, how much she discern. They don't know she know *they* hearts.

I wonder what made them horses leave the way they did. On the news, they played a video somebody took. Them horses crossed Rowlett Road, and that ain't no low-traffic street, but they crossed it without a care in the world. I mean, they busted out that fence and ran pretty to the empty lot next to the Shell gas station across the street from they ranch. Them cars was going crazy too. Pulling over. Getting out. Snapping pictures like they ain't never seen no horse.

I didn't find out nothing about it till she was already in my yard, lost in that patch of grass. She showed up just like that, in the middle of my watching another black person die before the whole world. From the gap between my fence tarp and the ground, I watched her hooves prance up and then come on around the side to my closed gate and wait for me to open it, like she knew exactly where she was going. When I opened it, she come in like she was invited or something. Come right in and walked by me and went to that very spot she stuck in. I left the gate open for her to leave, but I ain't cut the yard in a while, so she still busy grazing.

"Guess you ain't going back to your people," I say to the horse from my love seat. She don't look up. She just keep with the grazing. "All right then," I say. "That's what you want."

This my first time ever living in a white neighborhood, and I knew I hated it when my wife looked at the real estate agent, smiled, and said, "Yes, Aimee. This is it. This is the one we'll make an offer on." She took one look at how the steps of the front porch ascended up and said, "Wow. First time I've seen something so breathtaking. I feel like royalty. Right, Ridley?" When we finished the tour of the inside and was spit out the back door to the backyard, I nodded my head. Something about the smallness of it, thirty by thirty in all, made me think I could live in this place. Be happy in this place.

Now I can hear the police sirens out on the street. I can't see no laws yet, though. Not from the alley. Not from behind the fence tarp. They ain't made it to me yet, but I know they coming.

Cole hate how much time I spend in the backyard, but she don't never give me credit for how it used to be. How I was for her that year we was dating and them first two years of our marriage. She don't never thank me for how quick I stopped selling drugs after we met. For how I stopped wearing cowboy hats and boots cause she didn't like it. Thought it was country. She don't never talk about how I had my gold teeth removed and got implants in the front to cover up the smallness of my teeth from where they had been filed down for the golds.

I do anything she wanted back then. She was everything to me. Didn't matter that she snore like a freight train or snort when she laugh. I ain't care about her turning her nose up at folks when we rolled through the hood. My sister called her bougie and my boys thought she was poison. And it pissed all of them off how she called me Ridley instead of RJ or Don Juan, like everybody else did. But ain't none of that shit matter to me. I ain't ask her to change nothing about herself. I ain't never wanted her to either. Them pretty brown eyes and that sugar-brown skin was everything to me. She talked proper and knew random shit and all that had me lost in her. She don't talk about none of that, though.

She hate how I done pitched this tent. How I took the love seat she threw out last spring, covered it with thick plastic, and put it under my tent. She don't like that I spent almost a thousand bucks on a waterproof TV and put it out here with me. That I run cords from the back porch and stay out here most of the time. That I bought a space heater to keep myself warm through the winter and a high-powered fan for the summer. I pass most of my time sitting out here watching animal channels and black men die or reading books about animals and black men dying. She think all I be out here doing is smoking, but she don't know. That she think that mean she don't know at all.

In my mind, I done spent too much time trying to change myself for Cole. Trying not to be Ridley Johnson from West Texas. Ridley Johnson who hustled his way to the ranch he always wanted. Who everybody knew as Don Juan the gypsy horse breeder. Who everybody knew sold the best shit in Lubbock. Who everybody knew always loved horses and ranches and who hustled, honest and fair, till he had his own.

Dude on the TV crying and snot running out his nose, and I'm having a hard time seeing him broke down like that. He trying to talk, tell his story, and his eyes look even more shook than they did when he was laying down for the police with his girl. His eyes sit far apart, like they trying not to be on the same face, and his tears coming back just as quick as he wipe them away and he stuttering out, “We wasn’t doing nothing. Creshia talk a lot. Fire off at the mouth, but she a good woman. Don’t deserve to die cause she say what she want.”

A woman, a older one, rubbing his back and telling him it’s gone be okay. But the dude crying and saying, “We was just walking our baby to school. Just trying to get our baby to school. Wasn’t doing nothing to make them slam us on the ground. Now she gone. She gone.”

Now I’m sitting here watching this news and this beast, waiting for the sirens to reach me, and trying to figure out how to make this world work for me. I followed Cole from West Texas to here after she got the degree her parents sent her there for. Didn’t nothing matter that day but her smile and how she was wearing it for me.

She’ll be back soon. Gone flip about the horse being back here if she see it. She flipped when I tore the fence down two years ago. That was right after Eric and Mike. That’s when I started trying to find myself. Trying to see myself without her. Without thinking about how anybody outside of me see me. Trying to go back to before I was born and be who I was fore any of this.

When we bought the house, the whole fence was some kind of Western, red-cedar privacy thing. Couldn’t see nothing that was going on with the rest of the world from our backyard, so I tore the back of it down, the side that face the alley, with plans of replacing it with a low, chain-linked thing. But I liked it open. Better than the closed walls in the house even. So I started moving out to the back, little by little. After that, my rebuilding plans just kind of tapered off and I bought the orange tarp and nailed it across the wooden beams from the fence to shut Cole up. The tarp being there ain't really bother me none. I put it up just high enough that I can see the bottom of things. Ain't completely blocked in. I can see some of the world happening.

After she left an hour ago, she called. When my phone vibrated on that table and I watched the seeds and stems I'd separated from the good herb vibrate with it, I knew it was her without even looking at the picture she set for herself when she bought me the phone.

I thought about not answering it. After she leave the house, she like to call and nag me about being in the backyard. She say arguments less uncivilized when she can at least hang up in my face.

But I picked up the phone, wishing she just let me find my peace in peace.

"Yeah," is all I said when I answered.

"You at home?" she asked in a voice—in a language I know she don't use when she at work with all her other accounting people. She sound black, like she used to when it was just me and her, like she used to when I'd take her to my black world and make her forget anything else out there.

"Cole, you saw my car out back. I'm sure you heard the TV when you got out your car after work and when you got back in to leave just now. You know I'm here," I said to her, and I could hear the irritation in my own voice.

I heard the sound of her sucking her jaws, a thing I used to like when we was still new. It made her seem so sassy. So in control to me. That's what I liked about her the most when I met her. That's what made her stand out.

When I first met her, back when I lived in Lubbock, back when I was with my people on the East Side, back where things made sense, she'd do it all the time. The first day I met her at the taco place on Ninth Street, when she was still a Texas Tech student and didn't know the East Side existed, I stepped to her, licking my lips like I was gone eat her, and said, "Excuse me, Ms. Lady. Can I holler at you for a minute?" She sucked her jaws and it turned me on in a way that none of the East Side chicks ever had.

That was before she knew me, before I begged her to marry me and promised to be a better man. That day, she sucked her jaws and rolled her eyes and said, "Young brother, you'll have to approach me better than that. Now, because you are so very handsome and possess so much potential, I'm just going to turn around and pretend to stare at the menu. That simple act will give you a chance to rewind and speak to me in a manner suitable for a woman of my stature."

The fat girl with her laughed, but I took the opportunity to bandage my ego and try again. I talked her into going out with me that night. At first, I just wanted to smash because she'd tried to embarrass me in that public space, but after we went out to that bookstore for coffee, my first time going to a bookstore for some coffee, I wanted all the cats from the hood to see that I was moving on up.

"Yeah, I saw your car, Ridley. Smart-ass," she said. "I didn't see you, though. I called your name. No answer."

I exhaled, but didn't say nothing. I knew where the whole conversation was going. It happened every day. It was her way of breaking me down.

"Let me guess, you outside." And then she added, "Smoking." She spat that last part like it was something disgusting. Like she hated it. Like she hated me. And I just sat there with the phone to my ear for a while, until I realized she had hung up.

We live on a street of nothing but split-level houses. Cole liked that most about the neighborhood when we was new. Don't usually find nothing like that in Texas. Said it make her feel like she living up North or something. Like she was something else. Somewhere else. Somewhere better.

Anyway, all the split-levels in this neighborhood got second-floor decks and folks like to hang out on them on nice summer evenings and look down on the neighborhood they think they done made. Everybody see everybody backyard from they deck. Sometimes I come from under my tarp and see Cole and all the other neighbors looking down around me but not really looking down at me. They be shaking they heads, like they disgusted, but all the time they be trying to keep they eyes off me. They been complaining about how they hate looking out at our backyard. How "unappealing" the tarp and the untamed yard is.

I was in the house filling up my water jug the first time the HOA dude pushed the doorbell and complained. I was minding my business at first. I wasn't even gone go in there. Cole done made friends with a lot of the neighbors. I don't know none of them, though. So I usually stay out the way when they drop by.

"Hi, Nicole," dude said. "You got a minute? This is kind of pressing." I recognized dude. He lived on the corner and was always jogging through the neighborhood in colorful bike tights. Real skinny dude with a red face from always lounging on his deck in one of them beach chairs, like he on a real beach or something. When he opened his mouth he sounded like a man trying to sound like a woman. And I thought maybe that's why he was there. That maybe him and Cole cool cause they got a lot in common.

Cole stood there with her hand on the door and looked down at her yoga pants and T-shirt, like she was ashamed of herself. She shifted her weight from one leg to the other, and I knew she was embarrassed, so I walked up behind her to support or protect her or something.

Dude's blue eyes shifted up to me, like he was really looking at me for the first time, and then he dropped them to the clipboard that he was holding in his hands.

"Sure," she said and opened the door wider. "Of course. Come in, Justin."

"No. No, thank you, Nicole. I'm fine out here," he said, all nervous.

After that, he said folks was complaining about the tarp and the backyard and my wife face almost slid off with embarrassment as she tried to explain that we was renovating. I just walked off. I wasn't gone stand there and listen to her lie. Listen to her explain herself like he was the law and she had been caught selling drugs or something.

When dude left, I came back to her. Tried to put my hand on her shoulder. Tried to remember the times we used to touch each other and make each other feel good. Like the time I took her to my land. Let her ride one of my gypsies. She had never been on no horse. I held my hand firm at the softest part of where her hip and ass meet. She was trembling a little bit, but she kept looking down at me saying, "Don't let me go, baby. Don't let me fall." And eventually, she stopped trembling. Stopped being scared. My hand on her made her feel safe that day and that's all I wanted to do after HOA dude left. But she pulled away and said, "See, Ridley? See?" Her brown eyes was watery and she looked like she wanted to cry. "We don't live in this neighborhood alone. You have to do something about the backyard. We're supposed to blend in, not stand out. I mean, the TV outside, the weed . . ." She sighed like she was tired. "It's like you do all these things asking for trouble."

I ain't scream at her that day. I had already done enough the day I stood up for Mike. I just shrugged my shoulders and told Cole fuck them white folks. Fuck a HOA too. We paying for this house just like they paying for theirs, and that was the end of that. We ain't really said more than two words to each other since that day six months ago.

I'm sure some HOA member done called the laws about this horse. I'm sure they done seen her, recognized her from the news. They done looked down here and thought the worst. Thought I was a thief and called the laws on me. That's why the sirens stop and doors slamming right outside my tarp.

I hear all this going on, doors slamming and crowds forming, over the TV news showing black folks marching for the girl who got shot this morning, the one I been watching die all day. I hear all this and still sit there thinking about how I ended up here.

My momma brought me up in the church. Did her best to raise me right. She was a single momma, just like most of my friends' mommas. And I know it broke her heart into pieces when she found out I was selling drugs. She didn't never criticize me, though. I'm sure she prayed for my deliverance. That's just how she is. But she ain't never criticize me or slap the money I give her out my hands. I think she knew the conditions that conditioned me, so she bargained with God and let me be. She named me Ridley for her father, who she hated, and she let him teach me to ride and appreciate horses. She said they was always gone be the thing I could look away to. Said black boys need two things: a man to help form them and something they can look away to. I'm gone always be thankful to her for that. Always.

She was glad when I fell in love with Cole. She called her a "good girl." Said she was what she always prayed for me to have. And I guess Cole *is* a good girl. I mean, as long as I was peeling away the layers of myself, things was perfect between us. I guess she thought she was helping make this world safe for us. But I should've known nothing was gone be right after that stuff with Trayvon. I should've known all our differences was just too much. That her parents being college-educated and where I come from clashed, like a desperate clucker mixing the wrong drugs together.

"What they doing to us?" dude on TV yelling. "Why they killing us? This got to stop! Creshia Boyd! She ain't deserve it! Her name Creshia Boyd!" And I get a good look in his tired eyes fore the camera switch back to the blond-haired news lady.

His eyes make me think about how losing your woman like that, not being able to protect her or make her feel protected, is unnatural. How I been watching men die for years now, but Creshia Boyd done died fore her man. How he on TV crying cause he couldn't do nothing. Can't do nothing, and ain't nothing more unnatural than that. Think about all the black women that the camera missed dying. All the black women that's alive and still dead. All the black women like Cole. All the black women like mine.

"Creshia Boyd," I say soft. And then I say it again and again till I'm yelling it over and over, and I don't stop until I hear somebody yell from the other side of the tarp.

"This is the police! Come out with your hands up!" I use the remote to switch off the TV, put my blunt out in the ashtray on the table, and stand up. I stretch my body, like I ain't been off the love seat in years, and I let out a loud growl cause my body feel good letting go of itself like that.

I look out toward the horse and step from under my tent. She ain't messing with the patch of grass no more. She standing there with her eyes on me, like she want me to do something. Like she expecting me to. I see her eyes asking me, *Ridley, what's the plan?*

"I ain't done nothing wrong, officer," I say, walking toward the horse. "This horse come here on her own."

And then I hear Cole voice asking what's going on, like she out of breath, like she just run up. I think about Creshia Boyd and how she talked at them police with her face on the ground. How she was louder than her man. How she looked like she had had enough.

"Ma'am, you need to get back," I hear somebody command.

"This is my house!" my wife yell in her voice for white people.

"My neighbor called . . ." And her voice trail off, like she can't think of nothing else to say. "Ridley! Ridley? Baby, you back there?" she yell all of a sudden.

Her voice panicked and I want to smile because I think about what she said about Trayvon and his hoodie. How we sat on the couch together watching the news, me with my arm draped around her. We was both shaking our heads and I thought we was thinking the same thing, and then she said, "These young boys better get it together. He shouldn't have been wearing that thing on his head." After she said that, we debated. I lost cause I still loved her.

"Get back, ma'am!" an officer yell, like he her daddy and done had enough of her mouth. Like he gone grab her throat and see his whole life behind him. Like seeing her can make him disappear into the past. Like she everything he hate about the world. Like she ain't nothing, and that make me want to defend her cause she mine and she black and his voice ought to remind her of that. And then her voice gone and I don't hear her no more. She ain't Creshia Boyd. She done moved to a spot where she can blend in. Be dead.

"We ain't done nothing," I say again. "You ain't welcome back here. This my property," I say. And I hear radios and cops telling each other to move.

My mind go back to Cole and how she done listened to that law. How she wanted to listen to dude at the door that day. How she want to obey cause she think that's safe. Cause she think she ain't got no choice. I imagine her standing back with her hands smashed together like she saying a prayer. Tears in her eyes. Hoping I make the right choices. Hoping we be all right.

And I think about the day with Trayvon and how I let it go, but how I stood up when she said Eric selling cigarettes was criminal.

That he shouldn't have being doing it. That he'd be alive if he made better choices. I told her it didn't matter. He didn't deserve to die. I almost put my hands on her that day. I *did* put my hands on her the day she said Mike didn't comply. When she said he didn't really put his hands up so he got what he had coming.

I couldn't believe she believed what she was saying. My beautiful wife. The one I'd shed anything for. But when she narrowed them brown eyes, pursed her thick lips, and gritted her teeth and said, "What do you know? You not even an educated Negro," I lost it. That's when all the stuff I peeled flashed before my eyes. I grabbed her neck that day and watched her eyes bulge and thought about my gypsy horses and all the drug money that bought them and the drug money that was washed clean by me breeding them.

I thought about saying goodbye to my horses and handing them over to Moochie and following her to a job where wasn't no horses. Where I *am* the horse. And I thought about my granddaddy and how he taught me to click my tongue to move them forward. How he taught me to rub my fingers in little circles just above they nostrils as a treat. How he taught me steer with my legs if I ain't had no reins. How he always said, "Don't never try to break them wild, RJ. You find a wild one, you let him be."

When I let go of her throat that day, I let go of her. We tipped around each other, until I eventually moved out to the backyard. I guess it was wrong of me to let go of my son too, but I don't know no other way to be at peace about all this. To let all this go.

I walk toward the horse, close up the space between us, and I run circles with my finger on the space just above her nostrils, and I swear she smile like my gypsies used to do.

"You come to me for something? Huh?" I ask. "Walked by all

these houses and come right to me." And I let my hands slide down her soft coat. She muscular, like my granddaddy colts and paints used to be. She letting me touch her, but she watching me from the corners of her eyes.

"I don't want you to peel none of yourself off," I whisper.

I let my hand go back to her mane and grab a little piece of it while I coo at her. "I just want to mount you. Get us out of here. Get us free."

And I'm a little scared at first. I ain't been on a horse since Cole and me married, but seem like the horse nod her head at me. Tell me it's okay. She gone let it be easy. I step one leg back and throw the other one over her in one good jump, and she don't move at all. She sit there, waiting for me to tell her what to do, and I look up and see all my neighbors watching and pointing and taking me in from they decks. I feel like they all seeing me for the first time ever.

I smile, wishing I had one of my hats, hoping I look something like my East Lubbock self. Like Don Juan, the gypsy horse breeder. I want them to take pictures of me looking this way. I want them to think of me like this if they ever want to think of me at all. All I been in this place is some part-time worker getting took care of by his wife. I want them to hold on to this part of me.

"We're coming in!" a voice yell from the other side of the tarp and the plastic start rattling like they cutting through it or something. I click my tongue against the roof my mouth and gently tap my heel into the horse side. Soon as she start to move I release my heel from her. Let her know I ain't trying to rule. Let her know she free. I steer her toward the open gate with my legs, almost asking her to take me there. Trying hard to let her know I ain't commanding nothing from her. Then I let my heel sink into her flesh hard enough to let her know we need to run, and she nod her head, understanding ain't no turning back.

When we shoot out the gate, I see all the police cars lining the alley from the corners of my eyes. Seem like they don't know the gate open on this side, cause ain't no laws under the carport. They all surrounding the tarp in the alley, but me and the horse making our way round the side of the house to the front. By the time we got they attention and they start chasing us, yelling for me to stop, threatening to shoot, the horse hooves hitting the street hard and fast and seem like we lifting off the ground. I'm on her back, looking to her, and she taking the street to the sky with a smile on her face, like this always was our plan.

TIPPING

I always knowed I had some of my momma in me. All that hell. All that hardness. The kind that want to make people suffer. And I'm sitting here feeling the same regret she should've done felt all her life. Ain't let that man see all my love for him. And now he can't see nothing.

I can smell myself. I don't stink the kind of stink from working all night at the bread company. That's a sweet funk that Chuck loved. I stink of woman and sex and throw up and death. Momma back in my room, trying to get my bed together fore I can lay down. I wonder if the kids gone get sick when my sister, Cynthie Ann, get them back to the house from school, and I tell them they daddy done gone and died. That I found him stretched out on the carpet, like he was playing possum.

I had just dropped them off at school when I found him. When I screamed and called 911. When my hands started shaking, like

I'd run into a lost lover. And every time I think about it, I want to throw up again. We was just now being all right again. When I found out about the little bastard girl, Chuck threw my favorite coffee cup at me. That was last year. I didn't tell Momma or Cynthie Ann or nobody. We kept it all between us.

I sit in the dark kitchen and twirl the cup around the table with my thumb. Kitchen always been the darkest place in our little duplex, and the deep-burgundy plush chairs and drapes covering the window add to the darkness. I always told Chuck that a dark kitchen make sense. I ain't tell him Cynthie Ann the one what taught me that. She was the one who learned to cook when we was growing up cause she try anything to please Momma. Anything to get on her good side. Chicken was her best thing, but she ain't never get to make the kitchen how she said it needed to be to fry chicken comfortable.

When me and Chuck moved into our duplex, she come out here and helped me decorate. Walked in the kitchen and smiled. Turned and looked at me with her curls all big and perfect and said, "Get to frying up a bird and popping grease all around, whole place turn hot enough to kill you. Drape the kitchen in darkness. Keep the whole place cool." I smiled back at her and gave her charge of that.

"Lettie," Momma call to me from down the hallway. "I'll have these sheets changed in just a minute. Get you on in here and let you lay down a little bit. Might help your stomach."

And it feel funny to think she in my room, going through my things. In my space, where me and my man she hated so much shared.

I turn my mind back to the cup. It ain't been the same since

Chuck threw it at me. I glued it back together, but I guess the cup shattered into too many pieces cause when I try to fill it with something to drink, it leak through the glued-together cracks. I know he wasn't really trying to hurt me when he threw it. He was a right man. He raised my oldest girl until this morning. She ain't never know he wasn't her real daddy. Seem awful to want to keep that kind of rightness all to myself. Seem like something I ought to let the world remember him for.

Momma come in the kitchen. She wearing a wig and her fluffy fur coat. Ain't took the coat off since she got here. She got to be sweating. Coat look real heavy. But I don't blame her none for not taking it off. She in a place that's new to her. A place she got to know in her heart she ain't welcome to. I can see her trying to fix her eyes to the darkness and find me. I see good in the dark.

"Can't sit here in the dark. Come on now. Get cleaned up. Them girls can't see you like this."

And I want to ask her why she here. How she come to be a mother all of a sudden. How she come to bring herself to me and Chuck place. The one she ain't never stepped a foot in fore now. But I hold my tongue. My words ain't been coming out. I'm full of tears and bile. That's all I got. She take a few slow, easy steps toward me and just stand there. She don't touch me at all.

"Come on, Lettie. Get on up." Her words hard and rough. She move her body back and let me pass.

I obey her about getting up out the kitchen cause I done always obeyed her. But I don't want to wash Chuck off my body. What I got left from him on me is all I got left from him in the world. I know I can't obey her on that.

I let her lead me out the kitchen. She keep her distance. Don't try to touch me or nothing. We step into the brightness of the living room. That's where I found him. The first thing I saw when I walked in the front door from taking our babies to school. On the floor between the coffee table and the new burnt-orange couch he bought for my birthday last month. On his stomach with his hand stretched out toward our screaming baby girl. She was crawling to him. Trying be held and loved and rocked by him. But he was reaching and dying. Wasn't wearing nothing but his pajama pants. Ain't have on no shirt or nothing. All his twenty-nine years was stretched out right there, wrapped in ghost-white skin that wasn't nowhere near the russet brown I was used to. Dying and dead and gone.

This morning, after we had already loved each other in the bedroom, we brought it on in here. On the floor between the coffee table and the couch. I straddled him and we ain't even worry about our babies walking in on us. It was so early in the morning. Seemed careless, but it was what we needed. Him on his back with his pants pulled halfway down and me on top of him holding my gown up against my breasts. Me owning him and riding him and trying to get back to loving him.

I turn my head and think about letting my body fall into my momma to keep from looking at the last place I saw Chuck. I don't want to remember him like that.

Momma turn her head away from me and say, "Come on. Get on in here and lay down. You be all right."

We walk into me and Chuck room. She done brought the little trash can from the bathroom and set it up beside the bed. I ain't been able to hold nothing on my stomach. Not water. Not nothing. I can't hold life in me with him gone like this.

She look around the room and rest her eyes on the mahogany dresser me and Chuck found at a flea market when we first got married.

"That where you keep your clothes?" she ask. But she don't wait for me to answer. She just walk over and pull the drawer open and start going through it.

All I can wonder is why she here and not my sister. Why she allow this cold woman to be here when I need a comfort. Cynthie Ann usually ain't got no choices when it come to Momma, but this here is different. She should've at least tried to fight for this. And I usually feel sorry for Cynthie Ann. Always been me there to comfort her when Kareem leave her and them babies. When Momma beat her and talk down to her. She got six babies by one man, and he ain't never really been hers. He ain't no good to her. He ain't no good to nobody. She ain't never knowed what it feel like to live outside Momma's house. To provide for her babies without government help. To have a man waiting on her at home. To have a man hold her in the morning—make love to her fore the rooster tell the world to wake up. Now I don't feel sorry for her. Partly cause she ain't here with me, partly cause she can't lose what she don't got—what she never had.

Bed hold one of the last real memories I got of a tender moment with Chuck.

I followed him to the living room and fucked him after all that tenderness, but what we did before the living room is something beautiful to hold on to. I got in from the bread company at about five thirty this morning. He was asleep when I crawled under the covers, trespassed over to his side of the bed, and rubbed my naked breasts and hips up on him. He like my bread funk, so I ain't bother to wash it off. Hadn't done nothing like that in a long while. So I just put myself on him and he woke up and put hisself all over me. All in me. All through me.

When he thought I fell to sleep, he kissed me in the place between my neck and my shoulder and slid out the bed and put on his pajama pants. "Going to check on the baby and get my girls some breakfast fore school," he say. "I'll take them if you want me to, baby . . ." Then he sighed real loud. "I'll do whatever you want," he say. And I believed him.

I liked how we did things. How we ran the house. He was in debt to me, and I was gone make him pay fore I showed him how much I needed him.

"Nuh-uh, honey," I say. "Give me a hour. I'll be ready when it's time. Just like always, I'll take them."

I could barely see his face through the darkness, but the moon shine bright enough through our bedroom window, so I made out some pain, some worry in his eyes. He stared at me for a long while fore he bent over me, and I knew to open up and let him bury hisself in the soft of my neck. And he did, with his mouth full of my flesh, my skin.

I just smiled through the darkness and put my hand on the back of his neck, holding him to that place for as long as he needed to be there.

"What you do with the sheets?" I ask Momma, speaking for the first time since the hospital. "What you do with my sheets? Chuck in them sheets. I need them." And I'm gone cry. I can feel it.

Momma stop going through the dresser drawers and just stand there looking at me, like she lost. I shake my head and lift it up. I'm looking in her eyes and she looking in mine. It's like we ain't never really looked at each other fore now. Her eyes set hard, but she don't look mad like she always do.

"What I'm gone do? What I do without him, Momma? Who I'm gone be without him?" I finally ask, but I don't expect her to know.

Her lips start to move and she put her eyes on her feet. "That's silly, Lettie. You gone always be you. Now, get yourself cleaned up," she say. And I hear something vibrate in her voice.

"I can't bathe," I say. "I can't wash him off me." I sound strong to myself. Ain't no tears in my mouth.

Momma hold her lips together and nod her head like she understand, and it's the first time I ever feel like she done heard me. It's not like that time she beat Cynthie Ann in the middle of the street with a bicycle inner tube. I used to think Momma hated everybody, but I knew she hated Cynthie Ann the most. Was jealous of her own daughter. Was jealous of all the men she wanted for herself but they couldn't keep they eyes off her daughter. Cynthie Ann kids watched the whole thing with the rest of the neighbors. I was staying up the street with one of my classmates and her folks, but Cynthie Ann was still living at home with Momma. Our neighbor Happy Jack called me and I made it in time to look Momma in her drunk eyes and plead with her—try to get her to stop, but she cussed me. Wouldn't even hear me trying to reason with her. Called me nappy-headed and ugly. Told me to leave or I was next.

This time she say, "Okay, Lettie. Okay. Can we least change

your gown? Put on a clean one? You want to be clean for your girls, don't you?"

My babies Tootie and Nene, they be here soon. Tootie, my oldest, she gone have a hard time with this. She seven and smart. She gone understand Chuck ain't coming back. He been her favorite always. When I threw him out and tried to teach her to ride her bike, she told me she hated me. She fell, and I didn't catch her in time. Told me I should've been the one to leave, not him. I changed my work schedule after that. Stopped working the noon-to-nine shift and started working the nine-to-five-in-the-morning shift. I wanted to be there when my girls was at home. I wanted to be woke so they would know me too. After that, we started doing better. They got to know me, but Chuck was still Tootie favorite.

Nene just fifteen months younger than Tootie, but she seem a lot younger in her mind. She little-girl curious and don't care too much about the working of grown folks. I doubt she gone know what's going on. She in the same boat as the baby, who ain't even making sentences yet.

I hesitate at first cause I still can't believe it's her here with me through this. Can't think of who idea this was. Why Cynthie Ann would leave her. But I finally nod and do what Momma say when she tell me to lift up my arms so she can pull the gown up over my head. I ain't got on panties or nothing, but I ain't worried about hiding myself. Everything in the world done stopped for me. It ought to stop for everybody.

And then it dawn on me why Momma here and not gone to get

my girls. That it's something Cynthie Ann trying to do for me in her own little way. My momma hated Chuck. Felt like I picked him up out the gutter. Never wanted to understand him. She like Tootie real daddy over Chuck. A lying, cheating military man she told me to marry when I was seventeen. We never made it to that, though. He moved on without me fore he even found out I was pregnant. Settled in California. Guess he started a family there. I went to Dallas to get over him. Lived down there with my momma's sister. That's where I met Chuck. He was fresh out of prison, living with the older man who raised him. Ain't never really know his momma. She give him up to a stranger—a friend of the family—a few days after he was born. That man was the only love Chuck knew before me.

I was barely pregnant with Tootie when I met Chuck. All of us—me, Chuck, Tootie, and the man he called Daddy—lived together like a real family until the old man died the same day our second girl was born. And then, chasing family, we moved to West Texas where I promised to share mine with Chuck. But Momma wouldn't help me give him that.

I thank Cynthie Ann in my head cause now I ain't got to worry about Momma with my girls. My momma ain't got soft words that act like a pillow when you fall too hard. We was little kids when my daddy got cancer and his midsection swole up like a grapefruit in his pants. When the ambulance man finally came to take my daddy to the hospital, she didn't ride with him. She sat in the living room and finished her whiskey. When we cried for our daddy months later, she looked at me and my sister and brothers, straightened the wig on her head, and smoothed the wrinkles out her tight-fitting dancing dress fore turning her back to walk out the door. When she was walking out the house, she said, "Y'all won't never see him no more. He gone. Dead. That's over."

"Momma," Tootie calling me and standing right in my face. Her face wet, and her eyes look like she panicking. I sit up and look around, trying to wake up. Trying to come up out the dreamworld I'm still stuck in. The world where Chuck breathing and I finally let him know I done forgave him. Then, I place myself. Cynthie Ann sitting in the chair by the window, trying not to look at nobody, and Nene standing behind Tootie, who standing right next to the bed, with no expression on her face at all.

"Momma," she call me again. Her and Nene climbing into the bed with me. Tootie trying to get me to say something. Anything.

Cynthie Ann nod her head toward the other room, softly put her fingers to her lips, and whisper real gentle, "Tootie, the baby in there sleep. Let—"

Tootie ignore her, like she ain't said nothing. "Momma, wake up. She said something happened to my daddy," she say, pointing at my momma. "Said don't wake you up cause you sad and Daddy—"

"I . . . I just wanted them to let you sleep. I didn't know how to say it, Lettie. Ain't no right way," she say.

And it hit me. She done handled my kids the same way she handled us. She done told them they daddy over without giving them no hope for nothing else.

"You had no right!" I scream at the doorway she just walked through. I feel one of my girls' body jump on the bed a little, so I open my arms and let her fall in without really taking my eyes off my momma. I ain't never raised my voice at her; ain't never seen nobody else do it without a fight. I don't know what come next. The not knowing keep my mouth going. "You had no right to tell them. They needed to hear it from love."

Tootie sobbing out loud now. "Where my daddy?" she chanting over and over. But it's like she ain't even here. Ain't nobody here but me and Momma.

My momma face look pained, like she been slapped and it done brought a hard thought to the front of her mind. I'm thinking she might answer Tootie. Like she might tell her Chuck dead. He over.

"Love," she finally say, and I know she ain't talking to my baby. "Love? Really, Lettie? You think that was love? Think you know love?" And then she start laughing like she nervous or sad, and it make me mad. Nobody got a right to laugh today.

Momma look uncomfortable in her face, so she set her eyes on Cynthie Ann, but Cynthie Ann look down at her lap. Momma look at me again. "You too much like me, Lettie," she say, waving her finger at me. "You too strong to love. You ain't loved him, girl."

I can't believe her words. Don't want to believe them. Don't even want to understand them, but I eat them. When I was old enough, I left running from Momma house and all the men that wanted to touch me and Cynthie Ann. Momma was always too drunk to notice and too mean to mother. She ain't have kind words or cut the crust off sandwiches or even make sandwiches. She beat us and called it discipline and she cussed us and taught us we didn't deserve love. I come from all that and had the nerve to be sad for Chuck when I learned his momma never wanted him at all. Made me feel lucky. Cause least my momma kept me.

But I just want one more day with him.

One more day. I'd tell him I love him, and he should be happy. I'd allow him to do good by that girl, stead of telling him doing the thing he need to do mean losing me. I'd tell him to do what his heart tell him to do, what he need to do to be who he need to be.

I feel tears tickling at my eyes, but I ain't crying out loud like I been doing. I put my face down and let the tears drop in Tootie hair and then I lean in close to kiss the top of her head.

Tootie hair smell like Pink Lotion, like freshness, like love. I take my time combing they hair and oiling they skin when I get them ready for school. I always want to make the world know somebody putting care in them at home. I make sure they have a good breakfast and snacks in they bags and they don't never have to go to school wondering and worrying about nothing. Don't never have to worry about leaving home early to find a man or anybody to love them. I don't never want them to be scared of life, like Cynthie Ann, and I don't never want them to be too hard for it, like me. And I want them to hug and be hugged by me and by they mens and by they children.

I feel Momma moving in close to us. She moving slow, like a ghost, like she floating in the air or something. I don't move cause she ain't moving angry. I'm thinking she gone let me get away with hollering at her.

I hear a new voice. One I ain't never heard before. "Baby," it say. And I lift up my head cause I ain't never in my life heard her call me baby. Still, I can't get myself to look at her mouth. I look at what she wearing and think maybe she ain't even in her right mind. I look down at Tootie in my arms and Nene curled around the back of my body. I shake my head and set my eyes on her again.

"Hell," I begin. "It ain't even cold enough for that coat. Ain't even winter. Hell. That's what you is. Hell. That's what you ought to feel like."

"I gave y'all I had—all I knew how to give, Lettie," she say real soft like a whisper and hard like the past. "I loved y'all the only way I knowed how."

And them words that ain't hers make me move my eyes to her mouth. Her lips dark like they ruined from smoke and liquor, and they trembling in a way I ain't never seen them do. Even with the red cracks running through them, her eyes look sadder than they do angry.

"I done lost a husband, but I don't know how you feel. I ain't never gave no nigger myself like that. Always thought it was too much. Too soft. What I said before . . ." She let her words trail off, like she ain't got none, and she fidgeting with her hands. "Love about taking everything a person be. Everything they do and moving forward. Letting them be something better," she say, looking over at Cynthie Ann. And like always, Cynthie Ann can't stay that stare. She drop her eyes. Momma add, "I ain't never wanted to do that."

I remember my daddy and his grapefruits and him dying and him promising us she gone be better. She ain't gone be clubbing and getting babies by other men after he gone, he promised. Won't be no more not coming home and liquor and cussing, he promised. And I always thought he believed it too. Thought if he said it enough, he could make her stay at home with us. That he could make her love us.

And then I think about Chuck and what he was and what he did, and how I held him in place. How he couldn't be better after he messed up. How I wouldn't let him.

"Nuh-uh." I shake my head. "You can't go there. You ain't earned no place to be no comfort to nobody. No wisdom to nobody." I can feel myself spitting and gritting my teeth. "Chuck gone." I pat my chest. "But that's mine to carry. I don't need your help now."

She tilt her head to the side and it look like her wig gone slide right off her head. Her face look confused for a second and then she just let it all go and that same face go blank. "Your man just died, baby," she say. Ain't no confusion in her voice. She sound like she got the nerve to feel sorry for me. Like I'm the pitiful one. "I'm here for you now. I'm the one here for *you*."

When I found out Chuck was daddy to a child that wasn't mine, I raised all kind of hell in our house. Threw my cast-iron skillet at him; that's when he threw his hands up like a shield and tossed the coffee cup he was holding. It slammed against the wall and I put him out of our house. He begged and cried and apologized and I kept my face straight and made like he lost my love for good.

After he come back, we made a quiet deal about it and that made things all right. I ain't want to be my momma and go out and make myself all right with liquor, rage, and strange men. That ain't holy. She ain't holy. I did right by my man and my babies and my marriage. We cut a deal. A good one. We was happy with it. We smiled at each other, and we made love, and we ain't talk about what he done. Sometimes I even looked at him and seen him before he was a cheater and I felt love and real happiness and we was all right.

Nawh, I don't need Momma pity on me.

"Where you was when I needed you all the rest of my life, Momma?" I ask fore I know it. "Where you was when all them drunk men you brought home was peeping through the keyhole? When we needed a comfort?" I say, sweeping my index finger from Cynthie Ann to myself.

Momma eyes get wide like she surprised, like I done told her something she don't know, like she done ever cared. "I . . . I," she say, shaking her head. "What you saying, Lettie?"

And her fake dumb piss me off. Make me want to draw a line of clarity like the line I drew in our bed to separate me and Chuck. I drew it the very first night I let him come home. I called him over after I put the girls to bed. They had been missing him so till I ain't know what else to do. When I opened the front door for him, we just stood there looking at each other. Him looking down at me, and me looking up at him. I guess he got it in his head that I needed his long, strong arms around me cause he reached out to grab me. I ain't let him.

I moved back a little bit. Just needed to let him know what he did wasn't over. I just opened one arm into the house and told him to come on in. That's when we cut our deal. I remember his face after I finished talking, while I waited for him to make his choice. His eyes drooped down and his lips pouted, like he was gone cry. I felt scared, like he was gone make a decision and it was gone be bad for me. It seem like he didn't talk for a really long time and then he looked deep in my eyes, like he was digging through all of me, and asked, "You want me to just act like my child ain't out there in the world?"

I studied his face. The frown across his lips and the disgust around his eyes made me feel something heavy, something that made me know what I was asking wasn't right. I don't know why it made me think about the day the old man that raised him died. Chuck grieved that man out in the open and I was his only comfort. He laid his head across my lap and cried like I had just gave birth to him. We sat like that for hours before he said all stern, like a man that hadn't never been broke down, "No matter what, Lettie, my kids gone have a father." And I was thinking of that when I cleared the guilt out of my throat and said, "It's the only way. You got to erase her in your mind," I said, pointing my index finger at my own temple. "She can't exist if we gone be. That's the only way."

And he nodded and accepted it. After that he tried to grab my hand and lead me to the bedroom, but I swatted him off and let him follow me there. I let him lay me down and touch me and make up with me, but when we was through I told him, "I'm not ready to be held by you. Touched by you. I need my own side of the bed. I need it to be mine. You over there, and me right here." So I drew the line and unless he was inside me, he stuck to it and I didn't change my mind.

I make my eyes as hard and as tough as I did that night Chuck come back. "You don't get to play confused till you sorry about everything. Sorry for Cynthie Ann looking for love cause you ain't never told her what it is. Sorry for how Daddy died without your attention. You don't get to be no comfort. You don't—"

"I gave you the best I knowed how," she say, raising her voice and moving closer to the bed. Her face look angry and I see Cynthie Ann wringing her hands the way she do when she know Momma about to lose her mind. "I wasn't born no goddamn mule with no goddamn book about how to be no wife and momma. I gave y'all what I had left in me," she say, patting her chest like she tired. "I still needed something for myself," she add in a quiet voice.

"Shit. Might've been wrong more than anybody want to admit they wrong, but I thought I was right about that boy. I thought he wasn't no good. I could see him tipping out on you." She almost whispering now cause Tootie cries done died out, and we talking like we know her and Nene done dozed off on us.

She said that when I brought him to her house for the first time. Soon as he walked out the door she said, "Nigger ain't no good." Chuck had been so nervous about meeting my family. He was a nervous sweater, so by the time we parked outside my momma house, his clothes was dripping. He wanted my family to be his too. He was perfect that day. When we walked into Momma house, she was sitting legs wide open on the edge of her velvet floral-patterned love seat with a clear plastic cup in her hand and a cigarette resting in the side of her mouth. She had on a dingy, white silk gown that showed everybody who cared just how saggy her old titties was. She ain't try to adjust herself. Close her legs or nothing. She ain't even speak to us when we walked in. Just sat there till I finally said, "Momma, this my husband, Chuck."

Chuck stepped around me and stuck his hand out to shake hers, but she just looked up at him and chuckled.

She waved a lazy hand toward the couch that matched her love seat and said, "Sit down. Tell me about you."

Chuck let his hand fall against his pants and smiled nervously. "Yes, ma'am," he said and sat down to be grilled and mocked by her for over an hour.

When I had had enough of her, I told Chuck I'd meet him and the girls in the car. And when I was sure he couldn't hear me, I let her know that Chuck and me could live in peace without her blessing. That's when she cursed us. When she said, "Nigger ain't no good. Gone hurt you with his tipping."

She come so close to the bed that her knees touching the edge. I hold out two fingers, telling her to stop without using my mouth. She look down at her hands like she nervous or something. She sigh real deep and say, "I guess I was wrong, Lettie. Chuck come in there that day, and I saw something ugly in him. But I guess I was wrong . . ." She let her words slide off into nothing.

But she wasn't wrong. She wasn't. She was right all along. Chuck was a tipper—a cheater and a liar—and even with all that, I couldn't walk away. I couldn't be how she always tried to make me be. I stayed with him and made like I was hard when I wasn't. And if what she say about love is right—letting a person be theyself, letting them mess up and move forward, grow from it, and still loving them through it is the right way to love—I'm the one been wrong all along.

I don't want her to be right about Chuck. About me. If she right about us, then she might be right about doing the best she could when we was kids. And that thought make me want to break apart and spill all over the floor. But I can't. I got three girls. One day I'm gone need to teach them about men—try to teach them, like Momma doing me.

So I don't say nothing. I just start shuffling my babies around so they laying on the bed and not on me. Cynthie Ann stand up with her arms pinned to her sides, but she don't move from her corner.

I slide out the bed and can still smell Chuck and sex on me. I move toward Momma. I want to kick and punch her for every bullet she allowed to be shot in her house when we was little—for Cynthie Ann being scared of life, for me being too hard to live soft, like a woman. Cause she ain't never give a damn about what she did to us. And I want her to be Chuck, so I can tell him how he broke my heart—how all I needed was a little more time to be whole again. How he cheated all over again when he took my time this morning. I want to tell him that all I need is another day with him to be all right.

But all I got is her. Standing at the foot of my bed, looking like a damned fool. All I got is her. Her breathing heavy and her red eyes daring me to make a wrong move. I stand there, looking at the eyes that watched me suffer my whole life, and wonder how she still here. Still alive.

MOVING THE ANIMAL

....

For Chumley

It's four thirty in the morning, and Nate finally rocking his way out the bed. Can't just throw his leg over and get up since the stroke. I been laying here listening to Chumley whine about a hour, hoping—nawh, praying—Nate wake up and let that dog out before he make a mess all in that crate. He make a mess, that's on me. I'm the one got to clean it. Nate right hand don't work good enough, and sometimes I get in there to clean and find dried-up mess from I don't know when after he done tried to clean it up. So I just lay here, cause Nate need to start understanding Chumley belong to him.

Dog won't hush with his whining. I try not to hate him, but he always messing something up. I get to feeling guilty when that SPCA commercial come on and show abused pets. Make me feel like I ought not yell at Chumley. Like I ought not hit him with the flyswatter when I catch him drinking out the toilet. Nate love him, but he can't do nothing with him. Everything on me. He wanted a dog. A Old English Bulldog. Specific like that. Wouldn't have nothing else. Almost cried when I suggested something little, like a Chihuahua. And I done had to do everything got to do with the mutt. I house-trained him. Taught him about his crate. Taught him not to climb on my furniture and to stay out my room. But he *Nate* dog. I keep telling myself *and* Nate that. Hopefully that'll make him remember how to talk and how to walk like a man.

Nate stroke caused a bleed. Bleed caused his brain to swell, and then come the coma. After a while, them doctors ain't see no signs of life in Nate and wanted they bed free, cause he wasn't gone be they success story. They come in that neuro ICU room and about near put us out with they big words and little faith. Satan. That's all it was. Satan trying to scare me. I knew Nate would come back.

"Make sure you put him on that leash, Nate," I say, cause Chumley like to slip under the fence to run with the neighbor horses when we let him out just before dawn. Our little rental duplex is situated in a real funny way. It's the only one of its kind—only duplex, period, on our road—and we kind of surrounded by farms and ranches. Our place back right up into a big ranch. A few horses live back there, and Chumley think he one of them. He always come right back after I call him for a few minutes. I get mad when I got to call him and stand out there waiting on him, though. He a dog. Ought to come the first time he called. On account of Chumley running off, Nate done took to closing his retractable leash in the door and letting him go out like that. Sometimes I fuss at Nate about being too lazy to walk Chumley like he supposed to, but I know it ain't that. I know Nate just ain't who he used to be. His old self done passed away.

"Nam," Nate say.

And I tell him to get the leash again, cause I don't want to tell him that I don't know what "nam" is. He get irritated when I don't understand him.

He take a breath, make a hissing sound, and say, "Nam," again.

I just say okay and hope he do what I done said.

I'll wait on him to take the dog out and come back to bed before I start dozing off again, cause I want to make sure he settle back in all right. I done become a true caregiver to Nate, even though my oldest daughter say he don't need one. I try to explain to my daughters that I'm all he got, but they don't want to listen. Seem like, cause he they stepdaddy, they seeing him as somebody they ain't got to be here for, stead of seeing him as what he done always been to them. Seem like they done forgot how he was there for us—homework, driving lessons, and to hold us when my oldest girl's baby died. And I try not to worry about them giving up on Nate. I done got to a point where I do what I can to make sure they don't give up on me.

I hear Chumley barking outside, but I don't hear nothing out Nate. That make me sad, cause his voice always been important to me. He always been real good with words. To me, anyway. We ain't college folk like my girls. Matter of fact, we grew up in the same West Texas town before we found each other in Dallas. I was lucky to get out the cotton fields, and Nate was lucky to get out his daddy church. We done since wound up in the country outskirts of where we found each other, and maybe that's cause the country always gone be in us. But none of that matter when Nate open his mouth. He used to be able to talk like he was from somewhere real. Like he was somebody educated. He always been humble and quiet, but when he talk, it was worth listening to. Now seem like he half a person. Can't even quiet his dog.

I get out the bed, find my slippers, and make my way down the hall to the front of the house. Nate standing at the door, holding the dog leash with one hand and holding hisself steady inside the doorframe with the other. I see him struggling to pull the dog into the house, but Chumley just standing out there barking at him. I see the red beads the light make his eyes. He telling Nate, *I'm the boss. I say when I come back in.*

I walk up behind my husband—his shoulders slumped, kind of slanted, cause his brain ain't firing the right neurons to tell him to stand up straight—and I pry the leash from his hand. It's not that he don't want to give it up. It's that the stroke done destroyed his hand and he done forgot how to loosen his grip. Once I get the leash, I give it a hard tug and grit my teeth and say to that dog, "Get your ugly tail in this house." And Chumley stop struggling and hunch his body like he scared and try his best to squeeze through the door without touching me.

I let his fat self escape to the safety of his crate. I shake my head and smile at how slow he wobble over to it, like he hurt and want me to think it's my fault or something. I watch Nate hang the dog leash back on the hook and turn his body slowly, carefully, and make his way back to bed. I stand there waiting for the man I used to know to break out from the stiff-limbed man moving down the hall, stand there so long I forget myself. And then Nate turn back and wave his hand for me to join him and grunt, "Moan, Old." Every time he try to say my name, say Opal, it come out "Old," and I feel that way, cause he ain't even sixty and done become a old man, and I ain't even sixty and done become his old caretaker wife. Before his stroke, Nate never called me by my name. I was always Honey. In fact, my kids picked up on it and began calling me Honey stead of Momma. Now I got seven whole grandchildren that call me Honey too. When Nate woke up from that coma, I wasn't Honey no more.

I smile and nod my head a little and close the dog crate to lock our fat boy in. "Okay, sweetheart," I say. "Okay."

It's a quarter till eight. Chumley threw up in his crate after Nate took him out this morning. Ain't no telling what he ate out there. Nasty dog eat everything from frogs to his own mess. Ain't no telling what Nate struggling to scrape out that crate. A job I know he gone half do. I'm gone have to deal with it later.

I know Nate mad about cleaning up the mess cause I hear him trying to fuss. It just sound like baby talk or mumbling, though. I imagine he done closed the dog leash in the door. I imagine every now and then the leash handle move, but Chumley must can tell by Nate mad mumbling that now ain't the time, cause he ain't made no barking sounds.

After I wash my face and brush my teeth, I make my way toward the kitchen for coffee, but the smell so foul I got to take a pause. It smell like something died, like the rotting hog carcasses we'd smell when a good West Texas wind blew through my girlhood home. I know Nate smell it too, cause he look up at my face, and I see all kind of explanations in his eyes.

"He did more than throw up," I say. "He messed, didn't he?"

Nate shake his head from where he kneeling by that crate, and it make me mad that the dog got him in a position that's gone be hard for him to get out of. My middle daughter say he need to be in them positions. That he need the practice. But she don't see the pain come across his face when he struggling to stand up. She think I spoil and fuss over him too much. Say it don't matter that I was the mean one before his stroke. I done paid my dues and served him well. She don't understand nothing about marriage, though. She gone always be single.

"Ick," he say and point to the door where the leash handle hanging.

"I can't understand you. Open your mouth," I say. I can feel the irritation in my voice. The snappiness of it. It can't be helped, though. He make me mad when he try to talk to me without completely opening his mouth. When he talk to me through gritted teeth. I know what Nate can do, and he can do better than talking through gritted teeth.

"Ee sisk," he say, allowing his eyes to bulge and gritting his teeth even more. I can tell he getting irritated right back with me, and even after three years of living with this Nate, him catching attitudes is something new for me. Before the stroke, he never even frowned at me, but now he seem mad with me all the time.

"He sick?" I ask.

"Eah," he say and give his head one hard nod, frowning, like I should've understood him the first time.

"Ain't nothing wrong with him but greedy. Done ate too fast," I say, and I think about getting down there on my knees and helping Nate out, but I know I can't. The Wobenzym and turmeric stopped working on my arthritis about three months ago. My joints, specially my knees, make getting up off the floor pretty hard for me too.

Nate stop moving his hand inside the crate and grunt. He look at me and turn his head in the direction of Chumley dog bowls. I see all the food Nate must've poured in the bowl before he even brushed his teeth and washed his face. The bowl funny-shaped, like a maze or something. Man who sold us the dog recommended it. Said it'll slow him down when he get to eating too fast. Said if he eat too fast, he can fill up with gas or something. Said that can kill him. But I don't think that bowl slow nothing down. Chumley still eat like he done lost his mind.

I stand there for a minute, looking at that full bowl, knowing it ain't like Chumley to leave one single kibble in it. Knowing I usually have to clap my hands at him so he won't eat the three big scoops we give him in thirty short seconds. I told Nate just last night that Chumley look huge, and we need to lose him some weight. He was laying on his back, right in front of where me and Nate was sitting on the couch. Laying down there begging for a belly rub in his own little way. I noticed how big he done got then. That white belly spread out all over that floor, like something spilled.

When I open my mouth, I don't say nothing about Chumley being sick or not. I say, "We need to put him on Craigslist."

Nate nod and turn his head back to the crate. "Tay," he say, like I just told him somebody died. And I feel bad cause I done made him feel bad. Like less than a man. Seem like I should know better bout making him feel like that since he had his stroke. Now I see what all he done lost, and I want to make up for it.

I have to remind myself that things ain't always been this way. I remember when we was young, in our thirties. All the girls was still at home, and Nate bought them a puppy, a Rottweiler. Named that monster Nico, and I made him put it in the backyard when Nico was six months old. I'm talking about a mutt that mess up everything. Even chewed up one of the cushions on my living-room couch. I wasn't raised in no place where dogs live with people. Where I was raised, dogs was tied up to trees in yards. My momma always called it nasty when people lived with dogs like that. So I got to complaining pretty early on about Nico living in the house.

When I finally told Nate that dog had to go outdoors, he hung his head and commanded Nico to go. Nico listened too. Did most things Nate told him to do. Nate had a voice that make a mountain move back then. That's why I felt bad when, a few weeks later, after I made him put Nico out, he go to feed the dog but found him dead.

I could tell it hurt him by the way he come back in the house with the unopened bag of food and just dropped it by the door.

"Why you ain't feed him?" I asked, and he grunted. I still remember the roll of that grunt, like thunder beginning, like some big disaster coming.

"Why you ain't feed him?" I asked again and got up from my seat on the couch to find him some scissors. I figured maybe he had a hard time opening the bag.

"He dead," he said and made his way to the kitchen. "I just need a trash bag to put him in."

And I think about that as his hand start moving in the crate again. I think about that as I listen to Chumley start to act a fool out there. I remember that as the handle of the leash start to knock around inside the door. And I say, "Sweetheart, I'm sorry. He just get on my nerves. I can't stand that dog."

I walk over to the front door, bend down and pick up the leash handle, and then open the door. Chumley stop barking and kind of jump back when he see me standing there. His tongue unroll out his wide mouth, and his short, stout body make him look kind of vicious. He almost two now, but he was a little bitty puppy when Nate found him on Craigslist and we drove out to Denton to get him from the breeder. I still can't believe he picked a brindle dog. Brindle dogs so ugly. Both of us done always thought so. I guess the stroke done changed that too.

"You thirsty?" I say to the dog. "You old worrisome mutt," I add, as I step over him and make my way to the hose out on the lawn. He lay down on his paws, and I think it's cute and disgusting at the same time, the way all his extra skin and fat gather together on the ground.

I smile when the idea come to me—to squirt him with the water hose. To punish him for making the morning so horrible for us.

I make sure the sprayer screwed tight, and then I turn on him. He stand up quick and make like he gone run but then just stand there like he daring me to spray him. "You don't want this," I say to him, but he take a careful step toward me anyway.

I squeeze the trigger, and the water spray fast and hard right at his face, and this fool dog open his mouth and start jumping all around to catch it. He opening and snapping that big old mouth like he having the most fun in the world, and after a while he start getting so choked up and tired that he can't catch his breath. I let go of the trigger and watch him till I know he all right, and then I have myself a good laugh, and I think he laughing right along with me.

"You all right, ain't you, boy?" I say to him, still chuckling. "You all right."

It's eleven a.m. My hand shaking cause this dog and Nate and everything. Took me a while to dial my daughter number. My fingers don't seem to be working like they should. Feel like somebody driving nails through them every time I touch something. They give me just as much trouble as my knees. Sometimes I can't even use them. I'm just glad I can dial my baby girl today. Some days I can't even do that.

Chumley got my house smelling like dog, and I'm irritated with Nate, cause it just don't seem like he trying hard enough to be whole again. I want him to lift up his shoulders like he used to do when he was my pastor. When he was my man. Nate wasn't never no tall man, but when he step in a pulpit and crack open his Bible, he hold his shoulders straight, not crooked, and he look tall enough to touch the sky. Now he can't even chain that dog up. I told Nate to tie that dog to the stake behind the house, but every time Nate come near him, Chumley run and get low, like they playing a game.

And the kids don't come by like they ought to. When Nate was Nate, it didn't matter that we lived out past the city limits, out on these acres, where they got to drive a pretty good distance to see us. They come out every Sabbath and listen to the sound of his voice. Now seem like I got to beg them to bring my grandbabies to see me. So I'm by myself. Only me to talk to, since Nate can't find his tongue.

"Where you at?" I ask my youngest daughter soon as she pick up the phone.

She a therapist, and I got just enough stress in my voice for her to know I need her. I'm thinking maybe she might hear that and come to see about me.

When she tell me she returning something that ain't fit her at the mall, I grunt, "Humph." All she do is shop and take back. Could be over here comforting her momma, but she out doing foolishness. Selfishness.

"You coming out here later on?" I ask after she go on about work and her kids and the bad traffic. And that question make her pause. Like she can't think of no excuse to get out of dealing with me. Like I done asked her for money or blood.

"Never mind," I say. "Y'all just act like y'all done forgot we out here. Ain't got nobody to talk to. Dealing with this arthritis. Your daddy . . ." And all I can do is sigh. "Just lonely is all," I finally say, before she start going on about how she'll be out here soon.

I want to tell her I'm getting tired. Starting to worry her daddy won't never be who he was before all this mess. This stroke. I want to tell her about all the things I miss with him. I want to tell her that sometimes I think I'm losing my mind. Stead I tell her, "When you get here, I want you to put this dog on Craigslist."

She let out a breath, like she tired and what I just said took everything from her.

Honey, you always say that, I hear her say on the other end.

"I'm serious this time," I say defensively. "I'm tired of taking care of him. Your daddy can't help me with him. This all on me, and I ain't the one wanted the dog." Then I decide to hit her below the belt, cause I know my health is more important to her than her own: "Plus, chasing after him got my bones hurting. Y'all just don't know. You don't come here enough to know how much pain I'm really in. I—"

Honey, she say, like she done had enough.

"I just can't do both of them. I can't take care of Nate *and* this dog," I say.

Okay, Honey, she say, sounding all defeated like I done won. *We'll be over as soon as we done. We can talk about it then.*

"Humph," I grunt and hang up the phone.

Nate still following Chumley around the coffee table with that stake wire in his hand, like some little kid.

I take a deep breath and let it go. "Chumley," I say as loud as I can without hollering. Both of them stop and look at me like I'm God or something. Like the next thing I say gone give them life or take it away.

"Go in your house," I say, pointing to his crate.

He drop his head, like I done hurt his feelings, and Nate do the same. They little game over. Both of them look at me like they pleading with me, but I narrow my eyes and say, "Now."

Chumley climb into his crate like I sentenced him to death, and Nate bend to lock the latch like some kind of reluctant hangman. And I don't care about being the bad guy. Ain't no dog about to run my house.

I sink back in the couch and pick up the remote control. Dog done had us so preoccupied, we done missed the news, but I don't even say nothing about that. I just grunt. Nate make his way around to the other end of the couch, and I watch him, moving with his hands out like he Frankenstein or something. Soon as he pass from in front of the TV mounted up on the wall, I flip through the channels until I find one those crazy shows white folks done put on the air for dogs. I don't turn around to see if Chumley done picked up his sad head from his paws inside the crate, but I know he watching. This his favorite channel. I don't look in Nate direction when I feel his body come down on the opposite end of the couch, but I know he looking up at the TV and smiling.

Clock say twelve forty-five. Time feel like it inch forward on hot summer days like this, specially since this done become life for us. Nate ain't never been no rich man, but he done loved me like I was his earthly obsession since the day we met. He been a janitor or cleaner of things ever since I done known him, and before this stroke, even before we found religion, I ain't never known a better man.

We lived together about three or four years before we was married. We both had failed marriages behind us, and he should've been as scarred from his as I was from mine, if not more. His first wife was a evil woman. But Nate was still able to love me from the inside out. Back then I saw that as weakness. Man before him taught me how to run around on people and forgot to show me how to love, so I ain't love Nate, and I ran around on him.

Never forget the night I fell in love with him, the night he thought I was leaving him cause I was a bird that wasn't gone be captured. That night was one of the only two times I ever saw him cry before the stroke.

Before we was married, we rented a little town house in Dallas. My girls was with us. They from my first marriage. Nate come to us when my baby girl was barely a year old. He latched on and took us all like we was his.

One night I took the girls out to eat with my lover. When me and my girls come in that night, my baby girl said my lover name. And I could tell something in Nate fell apart cause he flinched, like fists was coming at him and slamming hard against his face. But he didn't let on. Not to the girls, he didn't.

I was shaking when I shuffled the girls off to bed. My ex used to hit me. Had a hard time *not* hitting me. Nate was gentle and meek and kind, but my momma always said that any man got it in him to put his hands on a woman if she piss him off good enough. When I made it to our bedroom, he was sitting on the edge of the bed. His head was down, and I could see him kneading his fists against his pants.

"You gone leave me now, ain't you?" he asked, and I stopped where I was and just looked down at my shoes.

"You and the girls, y'all all I got," he said. "Nothing else to live for."

And I saw something so big in him that my knees almost buckled. Tears was rolling down his face, and he kind of slid off the edge of that bed down to his knees and scooted—no, walked—on his knees until he was kneeling in front of me.

He looked up at me with the most sad and beautiful eyes I done ever seen, and seem like he, being vulnerable and weak and walked on by the world, rose up and became something grand.

"I listened to you put them girls to bed, and I sat in here and thought about what's gone happen next." He sniffed, and I remembered all the things I liked about him. How I'd catch him staring at me while resting his fist on his cheek, all lazy-like. How gentle he was with the girls, even when they was having a hard time accepting a man in they lives. How when he smile, he do it shy and drop his eyes, like his smiles come by accident. How that was his reaction the first time my baby girl called him Daddy.

"Honey, y'all all I got. I want y'all till I die. I want you for a wife and them for my daughters, and it don't matter what happened, where you been."

I pulled that man up to his feet, but not before I fell in love with him, and he done carried me across all these years. Took care of me better than I took care of myself before that stroke caught up to him. Caught up to us.

I step out the kitchen in time to see Nate coming down the hall, dragging the stake wire in his hand. He walk right up to Chumley crate and bend down to open it. Chumley stand up in the crate and start moving around, like he getting ready to bust out, but before Nate unlock the door, he tell that dog to behave. He clear his throat and say real stern, "Ack white."

Chumley stop moving. Seem like he just calm down, and Nate open the door and hook the wire to him. Nate guide the dog outdoors to the stake, where he clip the wire on and walk back toward the house.

All this time I'm standing in the big bay window watching, cause I'm shocked by Nate taking a stand and this crazy dog listening. And just when I think I got my old husband back, just when I think he gone make it out that yard and come through the door and call me Honey, that mutt run for him. I know if Chumley jump him from behind with all his 125 pounds, he gone knock my husband down.

I'm stuck in the house. I can't move. Too far to make a difference in what's gone happen out there. I feel relief when the stake cut Chumley short and Nate get back to the door. But it make me sad that my man didn't even know about the danger that was behind him.

Chumley ain't happy about being left outside. Chumley ain't *never* happy about being left outside. He start barking and carrying on, and when Nate walk in the door, I say, "Just wash your hands and eat. We can't let him bark too long. You know that old nut down yonder gone call the police if she hear him."

We found out the hard way that a dog ain't allowed to bark outside more than twenty minutes. Lady in the trailer down the road into rescue dogs and hate Chumley cause he come from a breeder. She used to speak to us until she found that out. Called the police one day when he barked too long, and they come and tell us that it's a twenty-minute rule. I guess you can't leave a dog outside no more. Can't tie them to trees like my momma used to.

We sit at the breakfast table and eat our lunch in silence against Chumley angry barking. Just before I take the last bite of my sandwich, Nate forehead wrinkle up in a way that make my heart speed up. It make me flash back to the night he had his stroke. His forehead wrinkled the same way when he come down the hall and said, "Honey, call 911. Something ain't right with my body."

I was working on my sewing machine, patching up one of Nate dress shirts for service the next day. He walked through that door, and I saw the left side of his face sliding down, like a melting popsicle. I watched him fall to the ground, and all I could do was scream. That was the day I watched my man slip away from me. That was the day my whole life turned. Now his forehead wrinkling up again.

"Nisten," he say, turning toward the yard.

"Huh?" I say.

He clear his throat. "No bark," he say.

"Oh," I say. "Good. About time he shut up." I think about Chumley being quiet, how he a good dog for that. I hurry toward the door to let Chumley in on account of his going quiet. You got to reward him when he done good. I'm gone give him one of his beefy treats. I'm gone let him sit on the couch between me and Nate so he can watch his channel while we rub his back from both sides. I know he'll like that.

"Chumley!" I call out, expecting him to come charging toward me, knowing I'm coming to set him free. But when I set eyes on him, he laying on his side with his tongue hanging out his mouth.

I'm confused at first. Chumley don't never relax like that in the yard. Then I make out how fast he breathing. The closer I step to him, the more I hear the struggle, the gurgling of his breath. I blink, and he ain't Chumley no more. He Nate down on the ground like that. He fighting for his life and he know it ain't gone be the same. We both do. And I scream and drop to my knees. That's when I see how swelled his belly is. I put my head on him and start talking to him: "Nate. Chumley. Get up."

And I think about him being out there with that big belly and no water and no us, and it finally dawn on me. I scream for Nate to bring me a pitcher of water. I look for anger in Chumley eyes, but they look the same as they did this morning. They look like *thank-yous* and *good-byes* and *love*, and that make me regret the flyswatter and all the times I complained.

When I look up, I see a blurry image of my man going fast as he can, with his hands out and water from the pitcher splashing all over.

By the time he make it to me, the pitcher halfway empty, but I take it anyway. "He thirsty," I say to Nate when he kneel down beside me. "He done passed out cause he thirsty," I say, trying to make myself believe it.

I start pouring the water in his open mouth, and I think about this morning when he was jumping for it, playing with it. I pray a silent prayer to a God that ain't listened to me since before my husband's fall, and I ask for this dog life, for Nate life, for mine.

Chumley ain't taking the water; it's just flowing out the side of his open mouth, so I drop the pitcher and lay my head on his belly again. "Nate, it ain't working. What's wrong with him?" I ask. And I wish my husband was the man he used to be. The one who would hold me and tell me that everything'll be all right.

I feel his hand on my shoulder, trying to be a comfort, but he can't say nothing. His eyes glassy, like he want to cry. It remind me of the day our first grandchild died. We all loved that little girl. When she was a year old, she got sick. Wasn't nothing long and drawn out, just a little overnight illness. It was the second time I saw Nate cry. He took care of everything had to do with the baby's death and everything had to do with us. When I saw tears rolling down his face at church a few months after we lost her, I knew he had held it all that time. That he had made sure everything was taken care of before he allowed hisself to cry.

It was like now. He patting my back, and letting my tears roll first. And he like old Nate—before-the-stroke Nate. And I know it's small, but I am grateful for it.

"We need to get a sheet, Nate," I say. "We can roll his body on it and try to get him to the car. We got to get him to the doctor." He nod his head, and I turn back to the dog. His mouth fall open and his tongue roll out.

Nate walking toward the house for the sheet when Chumley chest stop moving. I put my head on him, and I cry out, "No!" I don't feel no life from him.

Nate kneel down beside me again and pull my body away from Chumley. He ain't saying nothing, but he pull me toward him. He patting my back and rubbing my hair, and he ain't saying nothing with his mouth, but he taking care of me. And I know he gone take care of everything best as he can.

VIGIL

Elvis dead and Thala sitting on the couch with her legs stretched open. One of her knees arched up into a triangle, and the other laying on the couch like she want to sit Indian style. Her nightshirt sliding up past her hips. She ain't wearing no panties, and she ain't trying to hide it. I'm thankful for the dimness in the room. Her secrets seem dark as a old cave from where I'm sitting across from her. Mysterious and abandoned. She smell sour. Not unclean but not clean neither. Like what I imagine the sea to be like on a still day. Like seaweed gathered on a shore.

"But he is my brother," she whine into the phone in her English that almost ain't English, and I wonder how she do that. Thala ain't never been to Africa—her people's land—but her words don't say that. Sound like she done lived in a world with only them—Nigerians. Here I am done lived around white folks my whole life and still can't sound like them.

"I *am* a good Muslim. I am, you see. But I want to see him this last time," she say. I hear her husband voice say something—yell something—on the other end of the phone. His words really ain't English. They Yoruba or whatever language they speak.

Her tears make me feel uncomfortable. I wipe at nothing on my jeans. Then I let my eyes look around Thala's living room. The walls bare, but her furniture nice. The legs on both of her couches look like big wooden claws and the backs high like thrones. Like kings and queens live in here. The furniture too big for the little room. Ain't no space left for a television or stand or plant or nothing. The parts of the carpet I can see—the parts that the furniture don't hide—are stained with old spills that done turned black cause they ain't been cleaned up right. Her living room don't feel homey to me; it's clean, except for the stained carpet, but it don't feel like nobody home.

This my first time coming to her apartment. The last time I visited her, she still lived at her momma's house. Her husband, Wale, keep her busy. She used to call me once a month, but now she only call me on special occasions. Like today.

"I no longer have a brother, Nicki," she say, her too-big tongue making her words come out twisted. She ain't on the phone no more, but I didn't hear her get off—say bye.

I don't know what to say. Don't know why I'm the only one here. Thala and me, we done known each other since our high school days, but we ain't never been best friends. Didn't never get to be that.

I try not to think about her brother, Elvis. His always-dry skin, cracked lips, and perfect-white teeth. I try not to think about his growing, lanky frame folding over the dazzling women in traditional African dresses at Thala's wedding last year. It's hard. His face was so big and long and always there.

"Where Wale?" I ask after a while.

"He's with La Mare," she say, letting all her words smash into each other. "He had to get Elvis ready for to—"

"Put your leg down," I say, waving my finger in the direction of her knee. "You showing all your business, girl." I smile. I want her to know I ain't judging her. I think about how much she must sit there showing off the flowering private of herself, wanting Wale to look. I think about how much he probably ignore her.

I talk about Wale to my sisters. We discuss him and La Mare. How they—two handsome men—don't want twat. The stuff Thala shared with me—the things she used to share with me when we spoke once a month. My older sister said she'd beat Wale and La Mare's asses. But I didn't say nothing. Tried not to judge. Tried to be the supportive friend. Like Thala had been when I went through all that mess with Jude.

Thala and me ain't close enough for me to tell her that her husband supposed to come home to her at night. Snuggle up to her at night. Not with his best friend, La Mare. La Mare who lived with them the first three months of their marriage. La Mare who slept on their couch while Wale slept on the floor close to him. Wale didn't even sleep in what Thala call their "matrimonial bed" until after La Mare left. Now he don't come home most nights.

Thala smile and let her leg slide down. She run her hand over her hair. It look like she haven't combed it in days. "Sorry," she say. "I should be wearing a wrapper. The baby, when she was crying, she distracted me—"

"I understand, Thala," I say. "You got a lot on your mind. I just don't want nobody to walk in and see you."

She smile. "Bless you. Allah will bless you."

I smile back at her.

When I found out about Jude's whore—his military recruit—Thala came to our townhome and stayed with me and the boys for a week. My vaginal discharge turned dull gray, and I found Ramona Johnson's driver's license under my bed in the middle of Thala's Ramadan, but she flew from Texas to North Carolina wrapped in a white sheet and rubbed my back and dried my tears between her prayers. She still lived in her momma's house then. Still had to lie about being my friend.

Her momma hated me because of my first son. I was still in high school when I got pregnant with him. Thala's momma told her that ruin was contagious. Nigerian girls don't have babies and then marry like us. She banished me from Thala's life, so our friendship had to be a private one. For so long we couldn't *really* be friends.

I called Thala and not my momma or sisters about Jude cause I knew they would judge him. I wasn't ready to hear how doggish he was in the middle of my tears. I just wanted somebody there until it didn't hurt so bad no more. He'd strayed before, and it hurt every time, but I wasn't ready to let him go. Thala didn't judge Jude for his affair, or his love child that followed, or his rush for the divorce so he could remarry. With each blow she smiled and said, "Bless you, Nicki. Allah will bless you." I don't want to judge Wale neither, but Thala ain't got to take what he giving her. She ain't no horse. Ain't no mule.

I think about that as she sit in the passenger's seat of my car. She say the mosque on the other side of the city. I'm a little bit pissed off cause I ain't mean to drive her there. I ain't got gas for all this. After leaving her apartment late last night—late last night when Wale finally arrived—I promised to call her on my way to her brother's burial. I meant to drive there alone. Make my gas count. But Thala cried over the phone and I remembered her with me in the time of Jude. Now she with me and I want to ask if she know about Wale and La Mare.

Even with the window down, I feel hot and stuffy in the car. I look over at Thala. Her eyes closed and her head resting against the headrest. Her skin look damaged and rough. She sweating and I don't know if it's the heat or the baby weight or the grief or Wale, but I know this ain't always been her. I let the window up and turn on the air conditioner. Then I sigh.

From the freeway, I see buildings. They look old and abandoned and scattered. I see a whole lot of green space too. I wonder when they gone start building out on it. Green don't last in Texas no more. Sometimes I wonder how it's still some left. Seem like maybe grass ought to be extinct. Everybody want a house outside the city cause the city is all concrete. Now the parts outside the city looking like the city. Green disappearing and concrete everywhere.

A little car that's been riding behind me get out the lane, speed up, and ride next to me. The driver, a thin-haired white man, honk and throw up his middle finger. I mouth *sorry* to him and throw up my hand like I'm waving or surrendering or something. I'm used to being honked at on the road. I'm used to being sorry. My sisters say I'm a slow driver, and the personality test my therapist at the free clinic gave me say I'm a dog. Not a Jude dog, but a people pleaser. The driver in the little car look a little embarrassed and speed off.

We reach a part of the city I don't know. Each overpass I go under is covered by chain-linked fences and folks pushing grocery carts or babies in strollers through them. I don't want to wake Thala. She look more peaceful than she done looked since I picked her up. But I don't want her to be late to her brother burial.

"Thala," I call to her. "Thala, I need to know which way to go."

She lift her head, looking around like she trying to place herself. "Uhm," she grunt, "you exit soon." She look at the road, and then she look up at the freeway signs. "You are almost there," she say, looking at me with her eyebrows raised. "That was fast," she say, looking like she gone smile, until her lips begin to quiver like she remember she supposed to be crying.

"You should've at least brushed your hair, Thala," I say, trying to take her mind off crying—off Elvis.

She shake her head. "No matter. It is no matter. I will have to cover it. You will too," she say through a shaky voice. She look at my hair. "Your afro will smash." She let her head fall back on the headrest.

I never been to a Muslim burial, mosque, or anything. I'm Christian. When my grandmomma died three years ago, we waited two weeks before we buried her. We had her embalmed to keep her fresh while we waited on family from all over Texas and everywhere to come say bye to her. On the day of her funeral, after her pastor shouted for us to come and repent, we all walked around the casket and cried and fell on it and passed out from grief. Then we went home and talked about how the funeral home did a wonderful job on her face and hair and makeup. Jude was there with his broad shoulders. He wrapped his arms around me and that's what brought my tears. Being held and loved and alive. My momma wasn't speaking to me, but Jude's shoulders was broad enough to block the whole world out. He was all that mattered.

I'll cover my head for them—thesc Muslims—and I won't tell nobody how I don't want to smash my afro, the first part of me I found after Jude.

"Your father, Thala. He ain't gone get to say bye to Elvis. He won't make it in time, will he?" I ask.

Thala shrug her shoulders and sigh. She don't open her eyes or lift her head from the seat. "It is no matter, you see. He can't come. You don't come back from deportation. Momma was still pregnant with Elvis when he left. Fifteen years ago." She chuckle, but tears wet her cheeks. She smack her lips. "Sons make you a big man. His second wife gave him four sons." She raise up her head and look at me with cold eyes. "Chief Etti lost one of many sons. He will forget my mother and her daughters."

When we get to the mosque, Thala pull a head wrap out her bag and tell me to put it on. She wrap her head before we get out of the car and I stand there watching, trying to figure out how to wrap mine. The way her hands weave in and out and all around her head confuses me. When she finish, the wrap look good and tight. I know I ain't gone be able to wrap mine like that.

"Come," she finally say. "Let me." She start pulling on the cloth and jerking my head, but when she finish the wrap don't feel tight at all. I bend down and look in the mirror on side my car. I'd be a African queen in this wrap. The puffy hair I was born with is hiding, and I think I'm prettier than I ever been. Maybe I'll wear one every day. Have Thala teach me how to wrap it. Maybe I'll set my afro free on weekends and be a African queen on weekdays. Maybe Jude'll see me in it and respect me and want to love me and the boys, but I'll laugh loud and free like Thala used to when she was happy. I'll tell him it's too late.

The building big and white and majestic. Ain't no other buildings around it and it got a big dome thing sitting on top. It look like something straight out of India. Un-American. Ain't nothing around it but patches of green grass. Like the building got a street all of its own. Feel like we stepped out of my car to India or Africa and I ain't me no more.

I'm tempted to rub the side of the building when we walk up to it. I want some of the magic it's making me feel. I want to see if Genie will appear. I want three wishes: for Jude to realize that he lost a good woman, for Jude to be a better father to his sons, and for me not be so angry with Jude.

A lot of people, black, brown, yellow, and even white, walking toward the building. I wonder if they all here for Elvis. I follow Thala and a lot of other folks to the side, and I wonder why we don't use the front door, where it's two big golden doors with handles that look like they the size of my head. I don't ask.

"Good Muslims say goodbye to strangers, you see," Thala say, like she know what I'm thinking. "Good Muslims honor the dead no matter if they know them or not." Her voice sound mad, and she don't stop walking or turn to look at me. "Some of these people come every day just to say goodbye to strangers."

Make me think about calling my granddaddy and thanking him for Thala and Elvis. He ain't Muslim. He halfway Christian. All the way in his mind. But that don't stop him from going to everybody funeral—everybody black—everybody on the east side of Lubbock anyway. Sometimes he'll make it to three services a day. Once when I was little, I asked him why he do that. "Why you do that, granddaddy? Why you go to folks' funeral and you ain't even know them?"

He was still a alcoholic when I asked him. He looked at me through his one good straight eye and his cocked one, and he slurred, "Everybody deserve to go home with people round. Theirs or not. People need people. That's heaven."

I keep following Thala through a narrow door that spit us out into a hallway. The hallway lit up and long and narrow like a hospital or a school.

"They hold class for boys at this mosque," Thala say without turning to me. "We must enter here. We can't disturb the boys, you see." She walk in front of me. Her caftan so large she look like a Persian rug. Even though I can't see them, I know her knees stick together like they glued that way, but her feet look like they running away from each other.

We enter a gymnasium. It look like where we played volleyball at in high school. Rows of chairs is separated by a part like Moses's Red Sea.

"Come," she say, grabbing my elbow. She pull me to the left side of the room. "Welcome," she say and bow a little to some other women standing at the back. They smile and bow back.

"Are you on your cycle?" she ask me.

"Huh?" I say back.

"Are you bleeding—your period?" she ask. She seem a little annoyed.

"Oh," I say, shaking my head. "Nuh-uh."

"I am," she say. "I can't pray for Elvis." She nod her head toward the front of the room. "I can say goodbye from here, but I can't pray when it is time."

It's more than fifty men surrounding two wooden boxes sitting on top of short pillars. I can see the still bodies, positioned head to head, wrapped in white sheets, from where I'm still standing in the back of the gym. They faces ain't wrapped. Elvis's face ain't ashy, and he look like he sleep. A girl in the other box. She look Middle Eastern. She young like Elvis—like my boys.

The men in the front watching the bodies all quiet, but from the left, where I stand, I notice the women behind them wailing and swaying.

A man directing the wailers—the mourners—the women—on the left. He wearing a turban and shouting and moving his hands like my momma's choir director. "Don't let them see you cry. They will not want to leave you for heaven. Please. Shut up." His accent thick and his words sound short and choppy and rude.

I look at Thala. A few more women won't pass the point where she done stopped. They standing and crying and pulling at their clothes. The woman next to me, a African, is crying, "I am finished, o," over and over. She stop for a moment and put her hands on her head and do a dance step fore she start crying again.

"Yes, Baba," I hear Thala say, and I look up to see her plugging one ear with her finger and holding her phone to the other. "Okay. Hold on," she say.

"Wale!" she shout toward the front of the gym, like we outside or in the park or at a zoo.

I look in the direction of her mouth and see her husband's face, his big eyes searching the left for her voice. He wearing a white cotton pajama set like the other men, and his eyes look tired like he ain't slept in days.

When his eyes find her face, he frown and shake his head. He touch the shoulder of the man standing next to him and lean over to whisper something in his ear. La Mare turn back and look at Thala. His long face is blank. He turn back to Elvis, but Wale make his way to us. His tall, thin body weave past the other mourners, and his strides wide and quick. If it wasn't for him rolling his eyes and blowing air out his lungs all hard like, I would think he anxious to comfort Thala—happy to see her.

Thala bow to him a little bit when he get real close, and he look at me and make hisself smile. He point a long slender finger in my direction and say through gritted teeth, "You are welcome." His words hard and his accent thick and real and messy. He look at Thala. Her eyes looking at the ground. "You should not be here. You are his sister. Why you can't—"

"My father would like to pray with him," she say, holding her phone out to him without lifting her eyes.

He snatch the phone and go back the way he came.

Thala eyes follow him to her brother wooden box where he hold the phone out in front of him and start chanting loud prayers of his own.

"We are not supposed to come," she explain. "The women in the family—we do not come. But I helped raise him, Nicki. I raised him here in America." She want me to understand. I can tell by how she whining.

"You want to leave?" I ask her. I kind of hope she say yeah. This is uncomfortable and I want to get back to my boys.

"I just want to be here with him for a while. A moment. We can leave in a moment." I wonder if she talking about Elvis or Wale.

Jude wanted me to get a job. He said he needed help with the bills, but he also said we couldn't afford a sitter. He expected me to be the homemaker and helpmate. He didn't support my education—the classes I was enrolled in at the community college. He told me once, "Don't you worry about a career, baby. You keep taking care of me, and you ain't never got to worry about taking care of yourself."

I was part-time at Movie Gallery the first time I caught him cheating. He came in from work, and I was wearing a maid's uniform I'd bought with my own money. We only had one son then. I thought Jude was happy—proud of me. Two days before, I'd handed my first paycheck over to him with a smile so wide felt like I broke my cheeks. I wanted to thank him for his happiness, so I dressed up in that maid's uniform and painted my face and practiced my French accent and did my kegel exercises.

He walked in that night to a sparkling clean and quiet home. Slow jams whispered in the background, and I was sitting at the dining room table with a duster in my hand. I was as sexy as a tired new mother without friends could be, but he walked right past me into our bedroom, where he peeled off his fatigues and left them in a pile on the floor. "Let me shower first," was all he mumbled when I followed him, struggling in the nine-inch heels I was wearing for him. He didn't look at me. In fact, his eyes danced around the dimness of our candlelit room like they was searching for something he knew wasn't there. He finally disappeared into the bathroom, clicking the door locked behind him, leaving me with the pile of his cigarette-smelling clothes.

When he came from the bathroom smiling and clean, I was folded up on the bed, broken and in tears. I was being a good wife when I stepped out of my heels, gathered his clothes from the floor, and took them into the laundry. I didn't know what to be when the red G-string slipped out of a pocket when I shook his pants for change.

After we leave the mosque, I can hear Thala's father crying and snotting through the phone. He making gurgling sounds and chanting Elvis's name over and over. He called all throughout the service and then again when we got in the car. I wonder if he even know his own son face.

"*Assalamu alaikum wa rahmatullah*," she say. "And Baba, call soon," she say in a hurry.

We ride in silence for a moment. We close to her area of the city—the area where it's easy to find international grocery stores and bazaars and Mexican ladies pushing grocery carts full of laundry or food or babies.

At a stoplight, I stare at a short, stout woman. She look plain and tired. She wearing a old Coca-Cola T-shirt and a floral skirt. I don't know if she Mexican or Indian or what. Her face look like one of them Inca heads they used to show us at school. She got all three items in her cart: baby, laundry, and food. Her eyes look sad and stuck, and it make me feel pitiful. A car behind me honk the horn to let me know the light green, and I'm hesitant about moving on like I want to take the woman and her cart with me.

I finally ask Thala, "You want me to take you home, Thala? Wale gone meet you there?" And I want to know because he jumped in a box minivan with La Mare after helping the rude director turn Elvis's body toward Mecca when he was placed in the ground. He bowed at me and snarled at Thala and jumped in the van like it was some getaway car.

"I must be a better wife," she say, like she know my thoughts. "I must be more Nigerian than this place," she say, waving her finger around herself. "I married a Nigerian man. I knew what it would be like. My mother and my aunties . . . they have all taught me."

I think about Jude and how I tried and bent any way I could to get him to love me. But I should have known we was gone end up the way we did. We married cause of the baby and cause Jude's broad shoulders made it so I couldn't see clear. There wasn't never a real proposal. I packed up and moved to North Carolina where he was stationed in Fort Bragg. He asked me to, of course, and my momma protested the whole arrangement.

"Nicki, you ain't gone see life right through his eyes," my momma said after I told her I was leaving. She looked at me through eyes that knowed a lot. "Please don't do this, baby. You the one I expected the most from. Too late for your sisters, but you . . . We can fix this: the baby, school, life. We can. Just stay here. That boy's the devil. Anything with a dick is."

Jude drove to Texas to get us when it was time. When I went into the kitchen to say bye to Momma, she threw over her shoulder, "Go on and ruin your life. I ain't got no baby girl no more." My sisters stood at the door, shaking their heads like my mistake was bigger than the ones they made before me.

Two weeks later, Jude and me was standing before a judge and exchanging vows while our son screamed for my breast in the background. To this day, Momma can't stand Jude. When we was finally over and I called her to tell her I was coming home, she said, "Good for you. Thank God you saw the light. Woman can't be a woman with some man standing in her way."

Wale and Jude the same to me. I think most men is Jude. Thala's father, La Mare—they all wear Jude's face. They blocking Thala's view.

"Is he really mad at you, Thala? He can't be. Your brother just passed yesterday."

She shake her head and stare out the window. Silent tears snake down her face. "Take me to my mother's house," she say. "The baby—she is there." I nod my head, but I don't say nothing out loud. I speak a thousand words in my head.

"Maybe you can come inside. I'm sure there are pots and pots of *egusi* soup, pepper soup, *jollof* rice, and pounded yam. All kinds of meat," she say, smiling with her eyes closed. She make a sizzling sound with her tongue and then wave her hand. "Any foodstuff you want. I know my aunties have been cooking and crying and praying all day."

"If it's anything like the food y'all had at your wedding, shoot yeah. Spicy and perfect. Man, y'all can throw down in the kitchen," I say, thinking about how full of food me and the boys were after Thala's wedding. Her momma hugged me for the first time that day. She thanked me for being there for her daughter. She thanked me for Thala's bridal shower and for never asking questions about her son's sickness. I know it was more than that, though. She was just too proud a woman to say, "Even though I kept my daughter from you, she ended up pregnant before her wedding day."

For the first time ever, I wasn't scared of the milky film that coated the woman's left eye. I was sad for her as she held the phone up high, pointing it in the direction of her daughter and Wale so that her husband could see his oldest child pledge her love to a man from across the ocean.

"That was a good day, huh, Nicki? A beautiful day," Thala say, looking out the window. "I dreamed of a roasting son in my womb that day." She laugh. "Wale was so proud. He thought Lola was a boy. He made me think it too."

I pull in front of her mother's house. I think about Elvis's body and wonder if he is used to the ground. The box minivan is parked in his mother's drive. There are other cars—older cars. Some are parked on the lawn and others on the curb.

"Maybe," she say and stop talking. She start to bend her fingers back until they make cracking sounds. "Maybe if Lola were a boy . . . maybe Wale would be happy. It is my fault," she say, looking at me. Her lips quivering, and I want to pat her hands, but she popping them. "I wish I could give him two sons at once. You are lucky, Nicki," she says, and I watch the tears that threaten to fall from her eyes.

"Thala," I say, and I sound to myself like I am about to tell my sons right from wrong. "This isn't your fault. God meant for Lola to be a girl. Wale should love her just the same. He should not . . ." I let my words trail off. I want to be careful. She has always said what I needed her to say. I want to do the same. "Thank you for never judging Jude. Even when it was okay—when he was long gone because he didn't want me. You never judged him."

She stop popping her fingers and wipe at the tears that have not begun to fall from her eyes. She turn her head and look out the window again. "I grew up with a mother and aunties who told me all the secret ways to please a man—private, sneaky ways to make him happy. Top of the list: give him sons. If you do that, he is always happy. The other things help keep him at home."

I listen to her words. To my ears, they sound backward and crazy. I gave Jude two sons, and I did everything he asked me to as a wife and he still strayed away. He never even gave me the chance to give up on him.

"Jude's a man, but you had the power. You had sons, Nicki. That's power. Me judge Jude? Jude? For what, Nicki?" she ask, looking at me. Her face is a sincere question mark. It confuse me. She sigh. "Jude did nothing. He isn't to blame."

Shock start to drip all over me. Is she saying that Jude's cheating is my fault? Me, her friend? I want to tell her that friendship trump all that cultural mess she believe. I want to remind her that Jude broke her friend's heart. "He left me with those two sons," I say, pointing to myself. I feel like I need to remind her that it's me we talking about. "He left me," I say louder.

"Jude's a man, you see." She chuckle. "He has a thing," she say, pointing at her lap, still chuckling. "He cared enough for you to hide his other life." Her face get serious, and she poke a finger between my breasts. "*You* did something wrong, Nicki. You gave up first, then him. You have to keep vigil to be a good wife."

The air leave my lungs. I grip the steering wheel and breathe in and out, trying to catch my breath. I look at her, and she stare at me like she is waiting for me to receive her words—to believe her words like she's feeding me Allah and *jollof* rice and a second-day burial. I'm speechless cause she serious and sincere. And I finally understand her silence about Jude. It wasn't that she wasn't judging. She judged *me* all along.

I stumble over words in my head before giving up and saying nothing. I did everything in my power with Jude. Thala know that. Her brother dead and Wale in love with La Mare. Thala know that too.

She smile. "Ramona has no sons." She shake her finger at me and say, "Jude can still be yours. The power is still yours, you see?"

I think about my momma and seeing things clear. I think about all of Thala's aunties in the kitchen cooking and crying and praying and not saying goodbye to Elvis.

I smile and nod my head. We quiet for a long while. I search the deep spaces inside her sad eyes. The whites is red and that look natural against her rough skin. Skin that's gorgeous when she caring for herself. When she sure of herself. When she know her worth. I read her eyes and know her. I think she doing the same thing to mine. I see her daughter years from now, cooking, crying, and praying. I see my sons walking away from their sons with G-strings dangling from their pockets. I see myself in the ground, wrapped in white cloth, facing Mecca. Ain't no mourners at my burial place. Not even Thala.

When I feel tears building in my throat, I swallow, shake my head, and smile. "I can't wait to eat some of this *egusi* soup, Thala," I say, opening the door.

"Let us go," she say, getting out of the car. And then she remember something funny about Elvis. We laugh about it as we walk toward the house.

We approach the house as Wale and La Mare come out and walk toward the van. Wale stop and bow at me. "Mama Todrick," he say, calling me by my oldest son name. "You are blessed. Allah will bless you for being what you are to Thala." His smile real this time and his teeth not gritted. And I notice him do something Elvis used to do at me all the time. He bend one of his skinny knees toward the ground and slide the other leg out in front of him a little bit. He look like a bowing horse, like the ones me and Jude saw when we took our oldest boy to the UniverSoul Circus when he was still just a baby. And I realize he bowing at me, like I'm something grand. And I know he think I *am* something grand and I know he think his wife ain't. For a long time, I done let that make me feel bad for Thala. Today, I don't.

I don't let myself feel sorry when he turn and snarl at his wife. At my friend. I don't even shift my eyes to look at her—to see how she taking all the grandness her man see in me. I keep my eyes on Wale. I nod my head and smile, and I do it without showing my teeth.

DOG PERSON

For Jules, Bigger, and Housie

1. Jules scratches at the back door and shakes me from my thoughts. Before he scratched, I was standing here, leaning against the kitchen counter, seeing Miles's tiny face over and over in my head. He was cooing and making baby sounds with his little mouth, like he wanted to tell me something, like he knew more than I knew, and I wanted my thoughts to stay on that.

But Jules reminds me that none of that matters anymore. That he wants to go out. He loves being outside these days. Starts to scratch and beg to go out as soon as we wake up in the mornings. Doesn't give me time to wash my face or brush my teeth. Today, though, I'm taking all the time I need. Making sure I take care of myself first. Took my time getting out of bed, made my way to the bathroom, took a shit, a shower, and did all my grooming.

I push myself away from the kitchen counter. "Okay, boy," I

say. "Let me get a cup." He tilts his big head to the side and slides down into a lying position, resting his head on his paws. His coat is shiny and gray. It's like hundreds of quarters or silver dollars. Reminds me of my father's old Catahoula, Rusty, whose red coat was always as slick and shiny as fresh-spilled blood, even though he never got professionally groomed.

I couldn't sleep after Phoenicia called last night. Hadn't heard her voice in a long while and I replayed it in my head for hours after she hung up. It was late when she called. Her voice was soft, almost a whisper. When I picked up the phone, she called me by my first name, something she's never really done. For the first few years of our relationship, she would only call me King. Said that's what I was. She took to calling me Daddy when she announced that I'd be one. I don't think there was ever a time she said it that I didn't jump from the shock—the repulsion of it.

"Keith," she started out, soft, slurred, and groggy, like she woke from her sleep to call me, like she was dreaming about me or something. "I think it's time. I think I'm ready," she said.

"What?" I asked her, trying to wake up—trying to understand what she was saying to me. "Ready for what, Phe? Ready for what?"

"Things I need to say to you, Keith. Things you might need to say to me—"

"Of course, Phe," I said. "Of course, we can talk." My voice was anxious. I know that. I should've been calmer. Like someone who forgot the life we had together, like someone who had other things.

"In person," she said. "Let's do it in person."

And I gave her the Blue Ridge address and told her I'd be here.

. . .

2. This place is old, but I agree with the owner. It has a "rustic charm." Reminds me of where I grew up. Sometimes I can't believe I'm okay with that. When I was young, I only wanted to get out of Hale Center. I wanted to get away from the plains, yellow grass, and dirt. Mostly though, I wanted to get away from my parents—my father and what it meant that I looked like him.

I pour yesterday's coffee from the small, four-cup drip maker I bought from a yard sale. Left all the high-end appliances and furniture in the old house with Phoenicia. I even left some of my clothes. Figured I'd eventually be back at home. This was supposed to be temporary, but she's managed to stretch it out for six months. Won't let me be there with her to be there for her, which leaves me to sort through it on my own.

Even before we crashed, there were signs that we could spiral out—let go of each other. I should've seen it coming when she stopped smiling at me in her soft way. Stopped putting her hand on my shoulder and rubbing it to let me know she was there. That she'd always be there.

About a year before Phoenicia got pregnant, she started talking—fantasizing about being a mother. One day we sat watching a movie about a couple having their first child and she asked me what type of mother I thought she'd be, what type of father I planned to be, and I should've been honest with her then. But I didn't want to lose her, so I smiled and told her I wanted a daughter and that we would name her Junior. That she would be exactly like her mama.

We started trying not long after. Phoenicia began tracking her cycle, her body temperature, and even seeking out help from professionals when her efforts failed. When she learned that she was capable, that her body could bear a child, she asked me to go in for testing. In my own subtle ways, I refused. Whenever an appointment rolled around, I was busy or sick or forgetful. Eventually, she grew frustrated. Started to complain about things that hadn't seemed to bother her before. Nitpicky things, like my beard. That it was too scraggly. She'd appreciate a neater trim. I wanted to remind her that she loved my beard, but I didn't. Instead, I reminded her of our love before the whole baby thing. How we jogged the same trail for more than three years before we finally saw each other, before she finally tripped over a shift on the concrete path and I bent down to help her up.

I even bought her flowers—tulips—and a card on which I wrote *I love you fast.* I thought that would mean something to her—the little joke we shared after I proposed to her only two weeks after us meeting.

It seemed to work. We got back on track. She let up and we moved forward. But then she announced that we'd made a baby. I knew then I'd been betrayed. In the weeks following her announcement, I struggled to trust her. To stay with her. But it dawned on me that I'd lied first. That I was the original betrayer. So I tried to let it go. Tried to ready myself to be what I thought she would need me to be in the times ahead.

3. The microwave dings and Jules lifts his head from his paws. He wants to eat. He stopped eating dog food when the fruit started falling. I was worried about him at first. The vet had scolded me for three years about him being overweight, but his refusal to eat his food and the rapid weight loss startled me. I thought he was dying. But then I started finding persimmon seeds, sucked dry, in the house and all around the concrete carport outside. There are other trees on the property. "Twenty mature fruit trees," the "For Rent" ad had boasted. But persimmon is the only fruit for Jules. I laughed about it. Then it became normal. My dog turned fruitarian.

I had Jules when I met Phoenicia. We lived in my Arts District loft together. Where I grew up, dogs living inside wasn't a thing. Rusty lived his entire life hooked to a stake beside our trailer. We never bonded, but not because of that. Rusty belonged to my father, who always made his ownership clear. I was never allowed to pet Rusty. To feed him. To look at him at all, really. The one time I tested my father—whistled at the dog and sang his name out sweetly—I ended up tied to the tree next to him. My father made me stay there for an hour, out there with the dog. He watched me the whole time, standing there with his whipping cord in hand, daring me to move with his eyes. I could hear my mother's muffled cries through the open bedroom window. I was six years old then. I never really looked at Rusty again after that.

I found Jules in a potato sack in the bushes of the park where I used to jog. The vet figured that a breeder had left him there to die because he was born with a slight case of Wobbler syndrome. "Idiots," the vet had said. "They only care about the money."

He told me I could leave the dog, that he'd call his Great Dane rescue friends, but I decided to keep him. To rescue him myself. To have what I never got a chance to have with Rusty. And it was one of the best things I've ever done. He's a good dog. But even if he wasn't, I can't imagine kicking him the way my father did Rusty. Depriving him of food. Tying him to a tree. And, at first, that helped me believe that I was nothing like my father. Would never be anything like him.

Phoenicia explained to me early on that she wasn't a dog person, that she'd been bitten by a neighbor's pit bull as a girl, but I assured her—made her understand—that Jules was the gentlest creature she'd ever meet, that he was a part of me. I'll never forget how she tilted her head and smiled at that. And she made an honest effort to get comfortable with him. To get to know him. I watched her body stiffen when she'd enter my apartment for a visit, scanning the room for Jules. I watched those plastered smiles and nervous laughs and it made me want us to work even more. Eventually, she started bringing him treats and thinking of him. Started reaching toward him, trying to love him because she loved me. And somehow, she found it in her to let Jules become part of our love.

4. I walk to the door and Jules shuffles his large body out of the way, making a path for me. He wags his clipped tail as much as he possibly can and lets his tongue roll from his mouth, panting and anxious. The heavy wooden door creaks open, and Jules whimpers, his anxiety at the closeness of his goal reaching its peak. I step aside and allow him to pass me, and I stand holding the handle of the door as he leaps toward the open landscape.

I still can't get over the beauty of this place. I step out slowly onto the covered porch and make my way to a porch swing that seems to have been mounted long ago. I've thrown a blanket over the splintered wood for days like this, but I like the worn, unknown history of it. Trees are scattered across the front, but mostly there's grass—high grass where I've found field mice and toads and even snakes.

Before Phoenicia, I was different. Thought I hated country life. I lived in the city to prove it. But even in the city, I preferred being alone. Spent most of my time working—designing software, trying to be more than my father ever told me I could be, trying to keep busy and forget that I left my mother with him and his temper in a trailer in West Texas. When I wasn't working, I was home playing video games or watching movies or whatever sport was in season. I also spent a good amount of time running alone or walking park trails with Jules. After Phoenicia, though, I changed. I haven't ran in years.

She was a counselor at a school for survivors of trafficking. She didn't make as much money as I did, but she loved her work, had her own things, her own ways, and she was determined to love me. I adored that about her. I adored that she didn't pressure me to talk about my family. Didn't look at me like I was something wrong when I couldn't. She bent into me and became a comfort when I'd go quiet on holidays. She made those times all right. Always watched my face to make sure I was okay, and when she noticed something off, like a frown or dazed stare, she'd say, *It's okay, King. I'm here.* And because she was that way with me, I let her lure me from my apartment in the city to one of the surrounding suburbs, and I was happy until she wasn't.

5. I take a seat on the porch swing and look back at the door, making sure I remembered to close it. The house is white and wood-paneled. The paint is peeling and dingy. The back of the house—the part that looks out onto the advertised twenty acres—is like something from a dream. I have neighbors across the road from me. A narrow, blacktopped street separates us. The house sits back so deep on the land out here that we're a quarter of a mile away from each other anyway. I've never formally met my neighbors, but I have met their black kitten, whom I've taken to calling Phe the Cat. Whenever I open my front door, she makes her way across and loops in and out of my legs until I push her back and retreat into my house. She's constant company. At times, even more so than Jules, who is so taken by this place and this freedom that he has little time for me. When Phe the Cat's around, he treats us as if neither one of us exists.

Jules is near the persimmon tree. A couple of birds are swooping close. I watch for action. The past couple of days they have taken to chiding him. He barks at them ferociously and jumps up, snapping at the wings of one of the birds. The bird squawks and flies up before swooping back down and pecking at Jules's ear. The other birds flap their wings, moving up to a branch on the persimmon tree. Jules barks wildly. The birds squawk. They are laughing at him, and he becomes annoyed and starts to dig at the ground around the tree.

6. After Miles was born, we were always exhausted and out of breath. It was so tiring that we couldn't even see straight. We took leave from our jobs at the same time because Phoenicia thought it would help us better adjust to life as parents if we did it together.

There were times I actually thought about leaving. Times I'd look at her sitting there, holding and rocking the thing I never wanted. The thing that was impossible for me, and I'd have to remind myself of how she'd accepted Jules. Of how she let him become part of us. Of how I could let Miles in too.

And I began to believe that we deserved to live without sleep. That we deserved the puke-scented clothing, the blown-out diapers, and her complaining about cracked nipples. We were deserving of all the chaos. It was an invisible lashing to our backs. Mine, for not telling her the truth from the start; hers, for getting pregnant with Miles in the first place.

I tried standing with Phoenicia as much as I could. I found her beautiful in that rough state, that no-time-to-take-a-bath-and-put-on-a-face state that the baby's needs created for her. I joined her by not shaving and only wearing sweats. But I couldn't bring myself to hold him—to do anything that required that.

Before Miles, before marriage, when my father passed away, Phoenicia knew I was feeling down. I'd been moping around my apartment, but there was no way I could talk to her about the man my father was. About how I felt about him. Telling her those things would have meant telling her about how I knew I wouldn't become him. About how the doctor had tried to convince me not to do it. About how I'd persisted because violence begets violence and I never wanted to be a man who crushes himself over and over again. Telling her that might've meant losing her, and I couldn't—wouldn't—do that.

During that time, Phoenicia came by one Saturday morning and said, *All right, King. Enough. I know it's your father, but we all have to go that way. You don't want to go to the funeral, so let's go away for the weekend. You'll mourn him by living. That's all you can do.*

I remember almost every detail of that day. The knee-length yellow T-shirt dress and sneakers. The serious tone of her voice. The way she stood in front of where I sat on the couch, blocking the TV and knowing she was doing it. When I shifted my eyes up to her face, her eyes held a concern that made me reach out and let my fingertips graze her naked legs. Let the side of my face softly rest against them. When she put her hand on my head, I closed my eyes and let out a deep breath. The warmth coming off her body was soothing. Made me forget about my father, and that dissolved the cold I'd been feeling since I'd heard the news. Caused a warmth to grow from inside of me. We ended up making love right there on the floor.

I wanted to do the same thing for her when Miles was six weeks old, when the fatigue and messiness that had become our life lost its shiny newness for her. When we began to argue about me not being "hands-on" enough. When her cute and excited *Aw, he's crying again* turned to *Ugh, he's crying again*, I knew we were in trouble.

Outside of doctor's appointments, we had little reason to leave the house together, but we tried. Like the first time we ran low on food after he was born and needed to make a trip to the supermarket. Phoenicia suggested we go together—we take Miles. It was a mess. He screamed all through the grocery store and by the time we made it home, Phoenicia was leaking milk. She decided I would go to the store alone after that. She apologized. *I know you hate the grocery store, Daddy, but it has to be done.* So grocery store runs became my task, and I'm sure Phoenicia felt bad about that. She thought those runs were torture for me, but that's only because I let her believe it. I never admitted to her how happy I was to get out and away from them.

And there was a callus growing between us because I still wouldn't hold the baby. She whined about me not stepping up. Not helping her in the ways she thought I should. After a while, she stopped whining and just seemed sad. She seemed so sad.

I wanted to do for Phoenicia what she had done for me when my father died. I wanted it to be the way it was before the baby, the pregnancy, before all of it. I wanted to shake her out of the funk and I wanted to finally be us again, so I planned a romantic cabin escape and called her mother and asked her to come down and take care of Miles for the weekend.

Phoenicia declined the whole trip. Said she couldn't leave Miles for an entire weekend. I felt like a fool when she shook her head, smiling down at the bundle in her arms, and said in baby talk, *That daddy man's crazy, right, Miles? What's he thinking? Not yet. That's right. Not yet.*

7. Jules took to curling up on the pillows at the head of our bed while Miles napped in the center when the baby was about two weeks old. Phoenicia was the first one to spot them that way. From the living room, I heard Phoenicia let out a loud gasp. It was a gasp like something was wrong. I rushed to our bedroom to find Phoenicia with her hand placed over her heart. Her eyes were tearing up when she looked at me, and I thought she was beautiful with the scarf on her head.

"It's so cute," she whispered when Jules rested his head on his paws. "They're like brothers. Jules is protecting the baby."

I don't know why I thought about my father in that moment. How he would've beat Jules to the edge of his life for going anywhere near his bed. For a moment, I saw his cord coming down on both the dog and the baby. For a moment, I remembered exactly where I came from. And after that moment, I smiled at my wife, leaned against the doorframe, and we stood there smiling down on the baby and the dog.

Miles was eight weeks old when I found him in the center of the bed and Jules at the head. When I saw the two of them lying there, Miles on his back with his limbs spread out like a starfish, my first thought was to run and get the camera. But I didn't move. I just stood there in the doorway and watched them sleep. I think maybe in that moment, I was happy. I thought maybe I could be a good father to the child. I thought maybe I could love him.

When Phoenicia crept up behind me, wrapped her arms around my waist, and nestled her body into mine, I felt the tension that had been building between us begin to dissolve. I hadn't realized just how much I missed being touched, how much everything had changed between us. In that moment, it felt like we'd recovered something lost.

It was an hour before Phoenicia untangled herself from me to check on them again, before she went back into the bedroom and let out a high-pitched scream. An hour before she discovered that our baby wasn't breathing, startled Jules awake, and shooed him off the bed.

When I ran into the bedroom, she was on her knees beside the bed, holding the baby faceup in her arms, extending his tiny body toward me.

Do something, she said in a soft, broken voice.

I stood there, trying to hear her, trying to figure out what to say, but I could only focus on the child, hanging limp in her arms. With his arms dangling like that, he didn't look at all like he was sleeping. He didn't even look like he'd ever been alive. I'll probably never know how long I stood there shaking my head. Trying to listen to her. Trying to understand what she was saying to me. How long it took me to drag my whole palm down my face, like a squeegee. How long it took me to move my feet and get the phone.

By the end of the day, none of it mattered. Not her screams and tears or the love we'd made while the baby was dying. We looked all around the house, as if we'd lost a thing that could be found with dedication. We looked under couch cushions and beds and behind open doors. We looked at everything, except for each other. We held on to his pacifier and blankets and puke-stained burping cloths. We held on to everything, except for each other.

After the ambulance, after the coroner, after everything, she was first to speak through the darkness that draped our home that night. I was sitting on the couch, staring into nothing, and could feel her when she entered the room from another part of the dark house. She flipped on the light switch and I flinched from the brightness. I kind of opened my arms so that she would know to come to me. Fall into me. Let me be a comfort to her. But she looked down at Jules, who was resting his head on his paws near my feet.

It was him. I know it, she said in a whisper. *I want him gone. I want the damn dog gone.*

I didn't really know what she was saying. Didn't believe what I thought she meant. When her eyes shifted back to mine, she tilted her head, and I remembered the day I told her that Jules was part of me. That if he was part of me, maybe one day he'd be part of her. I wanted to remind her of that. To tell her that we needed to hold on to everything. Everything. But she straightened her head, pulled Miles's blanket tighter around her shoulders, and flipped the light switch back off. I took Jules to the local animal shelter, explained the circumstances, and surrendered him to a seven-day quarantine.

The next day, a medical examiner's autopsy revealed that there was no drawn-out explanation, that the baby just died, that sometimes babies just die. And after the graveside burial, after our parents and friends left us alone to mourn and try again, I retrieved Jules from the shelter and brought him home.

When I walked through the front door, she was standing there in the foyer, looking at herself in the leaning mirror that I'd told her just a few days before would have to be moved when Miles started walking. She was wearing an oversized caftan and her hair was covered with a scarf. When she turned to face me, I could see the wet in her puffy eyes.

She titled her head, and I could see a spirit of relief pass through her face. Despite all the grief settling inside of me, I wanted to smile. It had been so long since she looked at me like that. So long since I'd felt important to her, and, in that moment, I needed that. I needed to feel like I was her comfort.

And then, becoming aware of his presence, she looked down at Jules. She gasped and a horror coated her eyes that made me look down at him too.

It was then that I really noticed how ragged and unkempt he looked, like he hadn't been properly fed or brushed since I dropped him off at the shelter. I patted his side and cleared my throat.

They—they don't really feed them well in there . . . I said, letting my words trail off as my eyes focused in on her face.

She smacked her lips and shook her head at me and then she turned down the hall and I listened as she took quiet steps to our bedroom and closed the door behind her. When I heard the lock click, I knew that whatever was lost between us would not be found for some time.

8. I hear the rumbling of a car motor and look up to see the small crossover we bought before Miles was born pulling into my drive. The driveway is so long that it could fit an eighteen-wheeler with its trailer, but Phoenicia doesn't even pull in halfway. She stays close to the road. I stand up from the swing, but I'm not sure whether I should go to her or let her come to me. I'm not sure about who she is anymore. Not sure who I should be when I see her.

She climbs out of the car and uses her hand as a shield above her eyes. She waves at me and then leans her body against the driver-side door she just closed. I make my way down the driveway to where she's leaning and stand beside her.

"You can come in or we can . . ." I begin, letting my words trail off as I take her all in. She looks good. Healthy. She's not as thin as she was before Miles. Even her face is more filled out and perfect. She's cut her hair. It's not shaved bald, but it's close and it suits her.

I smile with my mouth closed and she offers a sad, closed-mouth smile too. "Nuh-uh," she says, and nods her head at the car. I look around her and see the cracked window and peer through the light tint. There's a small dog bed in the passenger's seat and in it, the tiniest Yorkshire terrier I've ever seen.

I smile and look back at her. This time I show my teeth. I don't know what it means that the little dog is in the car, but it feels like she's healing, like she's moving toward me.

"Look, Phe," I say. "I should've—"

"We're both working through one of the greatest tragedies we'll probably ever face, Keith," she says, shaking her head. "There were so many things we didn't talk about. We got married so fast—I shouldn't have shut down. That wasn't fair to you. Even before the baby. I should've told you what I was feeling—every step of the way. Even before . . ." She lets her words trail off.

We stand there silent for a while. I watch as Phe the Cat slinks slowly to my side of the road and Phoenicia looks off in the distance at Jules and the persimmon tree.

"I never really thought he did it," she says after a while, nodding her head in his direction. And then she looks down at her hands, which she has brought up from her sides to fidget. "I was just so hurt. Didn't know how else to process what was happening. I mean, our baby was gone and he was just sitting there. Alive. Just didn't seem fair that he was alive and Miles . . ." She lets her words trail off again. She's frowning now, and I can hear the dog in her car whimpering.

"You can let it out, you know?" I say, pointing at the window. "No leashes out here. Pets get to be free," I say, pointing a finger at Phe the Cat as she makes her way toward Jules.

She shakes her head. "She'll run away. She thinks she's bigger than she really is." She half smiles and says, "I named her Bigger because of that."

I smile at her and we lock eyes in a way that we haven't done since Miles was born. She seems shy and looks back down at her hands.

"I—it's good to see you, Phe," I say. "I've missed you."

She nods her head. "Yeah. Me too."

I nod my head. "I get it, you know. I think about him a lot too," I say, looking down at my shoes. And I do. I want to tell her that sometimes I wake up to his crying. That I come close to saying, *The baby, Phe*. But I don't say that. I say, "I don't understand this, why this happened to us, but I wish we could—"

"At first," she says, cutting me off, "I just wanted you to do something. To scream or cry because . . ." She places her hand on her chest and it reminds me of the first time she saw Miles and Jules in the bed together. "And when you didn't, I was angry. I thought about your face when I told you I was pregnant. There was so much disappointment. You never held him. And Jules—you showed so much of everything when it came to Jules." She shrugs. "I needed you to show me something for Miles. To show that you wanted him. That you loved him."

I watch her shift her gaze toward Jules. "I was so angry with him," she says, her lips quivering. "With you," she says softly. "Thought maybe you never loved Miles because maybe . . ."

She lets her eyes glide back to me—down to my feet and then back up my body to my face. And I see it. I see what we know, what she doesn't know I know, in her hickory eyes. They're sad, like she's held on to something unnatural for far too long. Like she's ready to relieve herself of that burden. She parts her lips and I know what's coming. What she wants to say. What she thinks she should say to me. This is why she came.

I've kept my knowledge of what she did quiet because revealing it reveals an original betrayal—my betrayal. I cannot be a father, and I made that decision, and I made the one to keep it from her. And I've always known that it could end us. We won't make it if she ever learns my truth. And maybe I also know that if she tells me her part, if she speaks it, makes it real like that, we *will* fall apart. I wonder if she knows that.

I open my mouth to stop her even before I can put the words together in my head.

And then I close it.

I should let the truth set us free. I should set her free, because maybe none of what happened matters anymore, because maybe we can be okay. Maybe all of it is over because Miles is gone and that's forever.

She's hesitant when she opens her mouth. "I . . . Keith, I need to tell you—"

"No," I say, surprising myself. I shake my head. We can't do this. I can't hear her. I can't let her do this. "No."

I watch her forehead crinkle and her eyes become a question. She opens her mouth to speak again. "I just want to—"

Jules's barking interrupts her and I look out toward him. I know it's him and the birds. He sounds vicious and his growl is deep and throaty. I step away from the car and Phoenicia steps with me. I feel her palm on the small of my back and I'm assured that we can be okay.

The little dog in the car is going crazy. She's made her way to the driver's seat and her paws are on the window. Her barks are screams compared to Jules's, but I know Phoenicia is right. If the little dog was outside of the car, she'd probably be attacking birds bigger than her right along with him.

"What's going on over there?" Phoenicia asks, making her way back to the car door.

I squint my eyes, trying to close the distance between myself and the dog. I notice that he's shaking his head madly from side to side and something black is hanging from his mouth.

I begin to jog toward him. "Good grief. He finally caught one," I throw over my shoulder to Phoenicia.

"Enough, Jules!" I shout, approaching him. "Let it go," I say, finally hearing the soft whimpers of Jules's victim. When he doesn't stop, I yell, "Stop it, dammit!" And he drops his prey and stands with his head hovering over it protectively.

Phe the Cat lands with a thud. Her body is limp and small and bleeding. I drop to my knees and yell at Jules. "Move! Get away from her!" I command him, and I hear my own voice crack.

He lies down, curling his body around a fallen persimmon a few feet away from where I kneel beside Phe the Cat.

The kitten's body heaves up and down. She's trying to breathe. She's trying to live.

I look out in the distance and see Phoenicia approaching. She's cradling her dog in her arms. I stand to meet her, to shield her from seeing what Jules has done, but it's too late. She's too close. The smile on her face is fading as we both look down at Jules curled up near the struggling kitten.

I want to explain it to her. To remind her that he's never done anything like this before. To tell her he's a good dog, but I can't find the words. I close my eyes and search for them.

I'm back at our place in the suburbs. I'm standing in the doorway of our bedroom. Jules is curled up at the head of our bed and Miles is splayed out like a starfish near him. My wife walks up behind me and wraps her arms around me. We stand there like that for a while before she gently tugs me from the doorway. I turn my body toward her, and for the first time since before she gave birth, desire for me is in her eyes.

We end up making love in the hallway and then again on the couch. And then we lay there, me cradling her and her holding on to me.

Phoenicia says, *This must be what heaven is like.*

I kiss her temple and ask her if we will always be this happy.

She moans, and I look down at her and she looks up at me and says, *I hope so, baby. I hope so.*

When she gets up to check on Miles, I imagine what she sees.

And just like that, I know. In the same way that Miles would always mark a betrayal that we would never speak of, she will always remember the dog I love curled up next to death—being a friend to it. And because he's mine, she will always see that in me.

We both stand there watching Jules lick his paws. And we both know what it means when Phe the Cat stops heaving.

HOLLER, CHILD

....

Part of me glad my son in here and ain't out there where Don Earl can get ahold of him. Part of me scared cause I ain't never seen this wildness in his eyes. He always been the most beautiful boy in the world. Skin like dark chocolate and eyes like honey. Even when he was five, he was a grown man ready to take care of his momma. My baby always been something special.

But tonight, for the first time ever, I think he look just like the man that took half my sight. Eyeballs bloodshot. Look like somebody done scratched red lines in them with they fingernails, and his face got welts coming up all over.

I sat at the dining table looking at the front door for hours fore he come busting through it like some kind of storm. Sat there all that time with my lips wrapped around a Thunderbird bottle, telling myself this was gone be easy cause I know my baby. Now he here, I don't know how to say what I'm posed to. What I told my friend Brooks I was gone say.

She called me at work just hours earlier. Told me to hurry to her house cause Don Earl wanted to see me and was real upset. I told Brooks she must be out her mind, thinking I can leave work like that. The university dining hall busiest at lunchtime and leaving the serving line liable to lose me my job. But I went soon as the rush was over and found her and Don Earl waiting on me. Brooks eyes was wet and Don Earl's was too. That there scared me to death cause I know how dangerous the work out there at Don Earl's place can get. He got a junkyard slash hogpen. Little place where he scrap old cars and raise hogs. Sometimes Quinten work with Don Earl. It's always plenty for him to do out there.

When I saw them—my friendgirl and that grown man sitting there crying like that—I knew something had happened to my baby out there at Don Earl's place. Turned out, though, they accusing him. And they accusing him wrong. Now Don Earl and a whole bunch of other mens out looking for him. Want to hurt him. Make him pay for something he never could've did. I told them to least let the law handle it. Prove my baby innocent. They want they own kind of justice, though. They want him dead in a hard, ugly way.

"Whole lot of people out there looking for you, son," I say when I see he just gone stand there at the front door like a fool. Look like he want to go back out but know he can't. He don't want to come in either, though. Look like he stuck between good and bad or heaven and hell or something. He trying not to look at me, but that's kind of hard to do, cause the living room and the dining room the same room. He walked right in to me staring at him, trying to see his face. I just need to hear it from him, cause I know my baby ain't done nothing.

"You do what they say, Quinten?" I come on out and ask him. I ain't got to be scared of what his answer gone be. I know him. He ain't nothing like what made him. Nothing like that.

Don Earl girl always flirting with my baby. Call herself having a little crush on him. She ain't but thirteen. Really too young to know any better. My heart go out to her. She remind me of me, and that's what got me tore up in two. I want to be mad at her for letting her crush on my son get him blamed, but I know what it's like to crush on somebody you ain't got no business crushing on.

It ain't never mattered to me that Quinten come from the worst night of my life. Last time any man ever touched me with hisself or with his fist. Quinten daddy was the Sunday school teacher at Right Way Church of Christ. Forced hisself in me. Knowed I was saving myself for marriage. He the one taught me that was the right thing to do—to save myself. And then he took it from me. Beat me good and called me a tease. Beat my right eye out my head that night. Been wearing a patch ever since then. Folks look at me like I'm weak cause I just got one eye, but Quinten don't judge his momma by that.

When he was little, he used to bring his fingers to my face and rest them soft on the patch. Used to beg to see the empty socket. I used to close my other eye and let him explore my face till he was tired. Let him ask all the questions he wanted to, and I'd make up pretty lies for answers. He used to cry when I told him bout how I lost my eye on a fishing hook. Hated fishing and hooks cause he loved me so much. It's been just us. Me and my baby. He growed up early to protect me—to help me raise him up to be a man.

"Quinten," I say. "Talk to me. Tell Momma. What happened out there, baby?"

He don't say nothing at first. Just look at me real hard. He look like he want to say something to me, but then he shake his head like he trying to turn something loose on the inside. "Momma, you got all these lights on? Ain't nobody here but you. You running up the bill." He put his hand on the light switch next to him.

And I think maybe he right. It ain't all the way dark outside, and we do try to keep the lights off most of the time. And him thinking about the lights—conserving and managing our bills—being the man of me, give me some kind of comfort. I member when he was seven, and I was having a hard time finding a day job. He'd stay home all by hisself—all through the night—and didn't never tell his teachers at school. He was a good boy. A real good boy. Always done tried to be the man of me. Look after me. Called hisself my husband when he was five. I told him nawh. He can't never be that, but he can always be the little man of me. He the one come to me bout working with Don Earl last year. The lights was off cause my check don't always cover all the bills. He had just made the eighth-grade basketball team, but when he walked in the house and found me sitting at the table by candlelight, he give it up. His eyes was bright that night. He was holding his basketball in the loop of his arm and his backpack was on his shoulders. He walked in the house and flipped the light switch, and, when ain't nothing happen, his eyes scanned the dark room for me. I was just sitting there at the dining room table, watching him. I ain't know what to say.

He found me and the candle and let the ball fall to the floor. "Lights off again, Momma?" he asked. And I couldn't give him nothing but a sigh.

"Momma," he called, moving close to the table.

"I'm trying, baby," I said, and I couldn't control the crying in my voice. I was tired that day. Tired of struggling and not never getting nowhere. I didn't mean to show him that, but I just couldn't help it. "I'm trying to keep it all together, but Jesus . . . Lord, I just don't know sometimes."

Quinten dropped his bag, fell to his knees, and rested his head on my lap. "Don't cry, Momma," he said in a grown-man voice. "Mr. Don Earl say he can use my help whenever I got the time. We gone be all right. I promise we gone be all right." And I believed him, so I let him give up basketball to be the man of the house.

It made me proud cause everybody thought he was gone be so troubled when he was little. Took him a while to catch on in school, and he acted out sometimes. But when his teachers sent us to the doctor, and the doctor gave us the medicine for his attention problem, he was better. He was good.

Now, I just deal with the same stuff anybody else with a fifteen-year-old boy deal with. Teachers call and say he can be disrespectful sometimes, and he got caught stealing from the mall a few times. Quinten try to nickel-and-dime drugs, but I think it's just a phase. Boys gone be boys, and I'm pretty sure all this gone pass. He a good kid. Even with all that boy stuff, he still a good kid.

I move away from the table and bump it with my hip. The Thunderbird bottle wobble a little bit, but it don't fall. Me and Quinten look at it. He probably thinking bout the past. How Thunderbird was with us every night. I want to explain to him that I ain't drinking again, I just needed something to chase the demons away, but I can't. I ain't never told Quinten bout his daddy. Ain't never want him to carry them demons. Ain't want to curse him with knowing. So, for a long while, Thunderbird carried the demons for us.

I move closer to where he standing. "Don't you turn that light off, Quinten. Don't you touch it," I say, and I sound like I'm gone whup him or something, even though I ain't never did it. Ain't never put my hands on him, not even a light spanking.

His hand slide off the wall, but his eyes drop to the ground. "Quinten. Look at me, baby," I say real soft, trying to plead with him. "You a good boy. You always been a good boy. Look at your momma and talk to me."

The Sunday school teacher who raped me knew the Bible like he wrote it. He loved the Old Testament, the law. I loved that—that he stood for something. He taught me that ain't nothing change on the cross—not the laws anyway. He was thirty and I wasn't but seventeen, so I loved him to myself. I ain't tell nobody, not even God.

His name was Kenneth Gray Ross, and I thought he was beautiful. He was tall with chestnut skin, and his smile was soft and sweet as buttermilk cake. When he talked bout Jesus, I saw love in his eyes, and I wanted him to be my life. But I knew he was too old for me, so I kept my dreams to myself. It was just a crush. But when he invited me to the house he shared with his momma to help plan his Sunday school lesson, I lied to my momma—told her I was going to the library—and I went to him.

Quinten tall just like Kenneth Gray. Handsome like him too. He lift his head up and look at me, and his eyes ain't wild no more. They sad and scared and confused. I want to go and wrap him up in my arms like I used to do when he was little, but he rub his whole hand across his face and start talking.

"I love her, Momma. And she wanted me. She was just scared. Thought her daddy was gone be mad. I would've stopped if she really wanted me to, Momma. But I wanted her and she wanted me too."

He go quiet and I do too. I want to understand what he saying. Make sense of it in a way that I can report back to Brooks and Don Earl. Me and Quinten ain't never talked about sex, but he my son, so I know he know better than to do what they saying he done. I got to make them know that.

I nod my head. "So y'all decided together? She said yes all the way?" I ask.

He nod his head and say, "She wanted to. I know she did."

I smile cause I know my son, and then I ask one last time just for the confirmation. "So she said yes? You heard her say it?"

His face look confused. He don't shake his head and he don't nod it.

I feel my hands go to shaking. My nerves acting up. "Nod your head, Quinten. She said yes. You mean to nod, baby. You confused, cause everybody know a shake mean no and a nod mean yes."

He nod his head, like I got it, and I feel relieved. Then he start talking. "You got to understand. This ain't our first time fooling around, Momma. We always . . ." He let his words go and sigh. "Man, she wanted me. We was kissing and stuff and it just led—"

I block his voice out my ears, and I'm in Kenneth Gray place again. He telling me about how pretty my eyes is and putting his hands on my titties, and I'm liking it, and then I'm remembering what the Word say and I'm convicted cause it's wrong, and I'm slapping Kenneth Gray hands away and saying no, and he telling me to stop playing. He getting mad with me and beating me in my face with his fists. He gritting his teeth and saying, *I know you like it.* I'm screaming and crying and he tugging at my panties, trying to rip them off. And I'm trying to figure out how all his love turned to this. I'm trying to figure out what that mean.

And when I can hear Quinten again, I know.

He say, "She wanted me, Momma. I know when somebody want—"

I shake my head. "You ain't do *that*, Quinten," I whisper. "Not that. You ain't telling me you did *that*," I whisper again. Cause I don't want to hear it. I don't want to know it. There got to be some type of explanation. Some type of way for him to still be who he always been.

He drop his eyes to the floor again, and I think about what made him.

I flirted with Kenneth Gray just like Don Earl girl been at Quinten. Was being fast and grown and wound up where I wound up. God come for us in the strangest ways. I lied to my momma face that day. Told her I was going to the library and put on fresh panties cause I knew what was in my heart. Kenneth Gray knew my heart too.

I shake my head and put my palms together, letting my index fingers fall against my lips. I start backing up, moving back toward the table. "Nuh-uh," I say. "You a good boy. You my son." I pat my chest with my open hand. "I raised you to do right things. I ain't raise you like *that*."

His eyes still on the ground and that's fine by me. I don't want to see his face no more. I don't want to see what I know there.

I shake my head. I'm trying to understand all this, but processing it is hard. Quinten stayed on my breast till he was almost four. Would ask for it—just point to my blouse and ask for it anywhere. I nurtured him till he was old enough to stop on his own. I wanted to give him as much of me as his spirit needed to cancel out Kenneth Gray. He didn't never once bite me. Was always so gentle. Didn't never just go for my breasts neither. Fore he could talk, he would point at my chest with a question in his eyes. After he could make sentences, he always asked like a gentleman. Always waited for a yes fore he moved in close to my body.

I nod my head and ask, "She said yes, not no, Quinten? That girl said yes?" I point my finger at him and say, "Say it right now. Say she said yes."

He don't say nothing. Just keep looking at the ground.

My face is hot and I feel tears behind my eye. "Nuh-uh." I take a few steps toward him, till I'm so close I know he feel my breathing on him. "Not my son. My son wait for yes."

He lift up his head, and his eyes look so lost and so young that I want him to look down again. His hand go to his face and he feeling at the scratches and the welts and I can see his hand start shaking and his mouth start trembling. That's when I see something pass through him. It's like a spirit, like the truth or something holy. Silent tears start rolling down his face and I know he know too.

He shake his head. "She didn't say yes," he whisper and then put his hands up in a surrender. "But I swear she wanted me, Momma. She liked it. She did. I—"

I slap him so hard my hand sting, and I shake it to get rid of the burn. And I feel all the pain on his face inside of me, but I don't look away or back down. "Don't say that!" I holler. "You can't say that," I say, softer. "You can't be that kind of person. You good. You kind. You you, Quinten. You mine." I'm talking fast and loud in his face. I can feel spit spraying from me and my mouth going dry. And then I just stop. Close my mouth so hard I'm scared I done broke my teeth.

I start stepping back again. Away from Quinten. Away from Kenneth Gray. I keep moving back until I touch the table and he look at me with his hand on his face and his eyes almost closed into slits.

When Kenneth Gray ripped inside of me that day, I went silent. My mouth was open but wasn't nothing coming out. I was scared my scream was stuck in my throat. I wanted to keep telling him no. I wanted to keep fighting, but I just lay there, with blood dripping down my face, looking dead in his eyes, through the one I could still see with, while he pounded hisself in and out of me. I kept telling myself to holler. *Holler, child*. But wouldn't nothing come out me. He was saying something. Maybe talking sexy to me. I can't remember. All I could hear was the sound of his body clapping against mine.

When Kenneth Gray was done with me that day, when he had

got what he needed out of me, he yelled in my face, told me, "Get out." He was still on top of me when he said it. Still inside of me even. "Get out, you tease," he said and just put his whole hand over my face and pushed it to the side. And then he pressed his palm down on the side of my face and lifted his body off mine. "Nobody gone believe you if you tell them it was me. Nobody, you little whore," he said.

And I knew fore I left him cussing me that day that I wasn't never gone tell nobody it was Kenneth Gray that hurt me. I knew fore I left him that I ain't want nobody to know. But when I stepped out the front door of the house, his momma was coming up the walkway, carrying a bag of groceries. If I hadn't been standing there holding my eye, trying to stop the blood from pouring down my face, if my clothes hadn't been tore up and hanging off my body, if I hadn't been sniffing snot, tears, and blood, I guess she could've thought I was just some fast-tail gal leaving her house, leaving her son. But the way she stopped walking and her eyes widened, the way her mouth opened slack and she dropped her bag of groceries, I knew she knew what her son had done. So I just ran. Ran until I was far from that house, ran until Kenneth Gray and his momma was far behind me.

I lied and said a stranger attacked me on my way home from the library. Kenneth Gray momma ain't never come out bout what she saw. She ain't come forward at church a few weeks later when the pastor called for prayer over the pulpit bout my situation. Kenneth Gray ain't come to church with her no more after that, ain't teach Sunday school no more after that, and his momma ain't never even look in my direction. I was relieved when she stood up one Sunday many months later and asked for prayer for her son. When she said he was moving to Reno with her brother. That they had found him work there. I knew I'd never see him again and I was glad about that. I didn't never want nobody to find out it was him. I ain't want to be embarrassed—to be judged for being fast. Didn't want all the bad parts of what I did to come out.

And I ain't never imagined that I was raising somebody that would hear the nos and ignore them. That would hear the pain and hold hell in his eyes. I ain't never imagined that I was raising somebody that was gone make me look at the nos and wish to make them yeses.

But when I look up at him, it's Quinten, not Kenneth Gray. He still holding his hand on his cheek and now he sniffing like he used to when I'd get onto him when he was a little boy. I can tell it's gone be one of them cries that stay with him for a while. One of them where even at dinner he sniffling, even through his smile. He the baby I rocked to sleep at night and nothing I do can shake that from my mind.

I shift my weight and my hips hit the table and make it shake. That cause the Thunderbird bottle to wobble fore it roll off the table and make a thud on the carpet.

We both look down at the bottle and I imagine we having the same thought.

"Momma, I didn't mean to hurt her. I just thought . . ." he say and start crying like a baby.

He sound like he five again, trying to be strong and help me carry groceries across the field to our projects. He sound like he used to when one of the brown paper bags would tear up, and he was scared he was gone get in trouble for breaking my bottle of Thunderbird.

I shake my head and close my eye and think about when he was little and asked me who his daddy was. He smiled and said, "I'm glad you stayed, Momma," when I told him his daddy had run off and left us. I ain't never want him to know he come from something so ugly. He deserved to come from love, so I told him he did. Told him me and his daddy loved each other, but sometimes love run its course and you have to let it go.

Quinten was so sweet and precious, and his smile was so perfect. I never thought about him when I was telling them stories about love running its course. He was tiny and needed me so much. I think about his honey eyes when he volunteered to be Don Earl slave and how I needed him to be just that. I feel like with what I know, I should be able to let him go. I should turn him over to Don Earl the way I should've turned Kenneth Gray over. I think about going to the front door and opening it. Bout screaming, "He here. He here. Come get him. My son in here."

But I can't stop seeing his tiny body carrying our groceries. I can't stop hearing him call me Momma. I can't stop seeing his question mark eyes when he wanted my breasts. I can't stop seeing none of his little life inside my head.

I catch all my good memories of my baby and hold them until I open my eye again. Then I push myself away from the table and stand up straight and call out my child's name.

He try to pull hisself together, but he can't stop crying. Can't stop saying sorry over and over again.

"Pull yourself together, boy," I say through gritted teeth.

He wipe his eyes and try to stop crying. He heaving and it look like he struggling to breathe. I want to go to him. Be a comfort to him, like he done been to me so many times, but I got to make him know the way things is.

I point to the door he walked in through and say so low it's a whisper, "You gone say shit like that—say that girl ain't say yes—you get your ass on out of here."

He look back at the door, but he don't leave.

"Come here," I say, pointing to the floor in front of me.

He step slow and careful toward me till he almost right up in my face. I can tell he afraid. More afraid of me than he done ever had a reason to be.

I shake my head and open my arms to him and let him fold hisself into me. He start crying again and I can feel the wet of him on my shoulder.

"Shh," I say. "It's all right, baby. Momma here." I sigh and say, "Just don't never let me hear you say that, kay?" I peel him away from me and look up at him. Make sure he can see the tears in my eye. See how much this hurt me. I nod my head and sniff before saying, "She wanted you. You hear me? It was her idea. She said yes. She took your clothes off. She said yes all the way. You hear me?" I say.

I wipe away the tears from his face and he pull away from my touch.

He shake his head and say, "But Momma, I—"

Fore I got time to think about it, I slap him, and when his face turn from the one slap, I use my other hand to slap the other side, and then I ball up my fists and close my eyes. "Listen to me," I say through gritted teeth. "Listen," I repeat.

This time he don't cry. His mouth is closed, but I can tell he clinching his teeth cause the side of his jaw is twitching a little bit. I want to be gentle with him and promise him we'll get through this, but now ain't the time for that. I got to give him what he need.

I clutch his shoulders and shake them a little before I whisper, "Listen."

And I know I got his attention. He looking down at me with confusion and anger, or maybe it's fear in his eyes. And I'm looking up at him with all the words to keep him safe.

SWEAT

Lotrece woke up dripping sweat the night her marriage ended. The ceiling fan hummed above her and she could feel the central air-conditioning blowing full blast. The room was neither warm nor cold, which is why, at first, she thought she was dripping blood. Thought she started her period and then she remembered she no longer had a uterus from which blood could drip. That part of her was gone.

When she realized it was sweat, she looked over at her husband, Clayton. He'd kicked himself free from the covers, and the moonlight through their bedroom window allowed her just enough light to stare at the way the flesh around his center sagged over his underwear. It looked painful, and she almost felt sorry for him, until her eyes moved to the nightstand on his side. There was a half-eaten Twinkie, a tin container of flavored almonds, and what she guessed was a sandwich wrapped in a paper towel.

She scoffed and slid her leg off the bed. She was tired of lecturing him about eating in bed. About smoking cigarettes. About marijuana and how black it made his lips. How dingy all of those things made him look. *We in our forties now*, she'd told him. *Ain't like when we was teenagers. We got to be careful with ourselves. We real fragile. Don't keep as good.* But really, she just meant him.

She used her palms to push herself from the mattress, closed her eyes, and gritted her teeth when the box spring let out a wooden groan. She didn't want to wake him and she did. She wanted to tell him about his sweat. How it encouraged hers. How she wasn't a night sweater a year ago. She wanted him to believe what she believed.

Clayton had always been a sweater, except for those few periods of time when it temporarily tapered off. Those periods of time when he was making the right choices. He was a hairy man, but that wasn't it. His eating habits were terrible, he was a smoker, and he was a cheater. Lotrece believed that all of those things became ghosts in the night and came through his pores to haunt him and remind her of who he was. And when she thought of that, she didn't want him to open his eyes, to open his mouth. She was tired of fighting. He would be who he was and she would be herself. And that was that.

When they were young and he always smelled of expensive cologne, he'd tell her their scents blended well together. She believed him because his sleepy eyes were beautiful and his lips were pink and full. All she could smell now was her own faint oniony musk and his powerful, almost corn chip, almost feet one.

She stood on her side of the bed, the side closest to the door, and looked down at him. It used to be his side of the bed, until two springs ago when the cockroaches invaded from the nest in the attic. The first ones came down and climbed into bed with them. Always on her side. Never on Clayton's. She'd been appalled and offended at how the bugs chose her when she kept no snacks or sweat on her side of the room.

And he didn't offer to switch sides. In fact, he rolled his eyes and told her to quit being dramatic. *It's not my fault this is happening*, he whined. *Don't take it out on me.*

She moved out to the couch after he refused to trade places with her. She ignored him for three days, pretending that they were strangers passing through the same space. On the third night, he moved his things over to her side of the bed, and she moved back in. They never mentioned those three days and carried on as if his side of the bed had always been hers.

As she looked down at him, she thought about yelling and waking him. Telling him that she wanted her side back, but she didn't. She had no idea what she wanted. Sometimes she thought she wanted to return to something from the past. She had tried to request it in prayer, but she was uncertain about what the past really was and if she really wanted to return to it. She only knew what Clayton had become. What she feared she was becoming because of him.

She peeled off her wet gown and let it fall onto the floor. She let her thumbs guide her damp panties down her legs, until they were close enough to her feet to be kicked off. She closed her eyes and placed her palms on the flat of her stomach. She could feel her lips curling into a smile. Her body was her new pride. She visited the gym four times per week. Her ab work was anything but light. She told herself she had no choice. More than a decade before, during her thirty-second year, she gained twenty pounds and it scared her to death. She did not want that for herself. For him. So she worked at it.

She slid her hands up the dampness of her skin, until they were under her breasts. She cupped herself and wondered if Clayton might've been happier if they were larger, perkier even. She swiped her hands slowly underneath them, in opposite directions. She crinkled her nose at the wetness her fingers collected as she brought her hands up to her nose and sniffed. She opened her eyes and frowned at her musky scent. "Eww," she said out loud before turning and walking toward the bedroom door.

Last year, in what she now considered the old days, she would have grabbed her robe from the hook on the door, but the children were no longer children. They were no longer home. The baby, Valencia, had left for college last August. Lotrece hadn't expected to get emotional about her daughter leaving, but once it came time for her to go, she found herself trying hard not to cry. She reasoned that Valencia was the youngest child, the last thing she'd get a chance to mother, the very last thing they could look away to. After they packed the last box of Valencia's things into the tiny dorm room she was to share with a stranger, after she'd skipped out happily behind them as they made their way back to the car with the rest of the abandoned parents, Lotrece's lips quivered and Valencia must've saw it. Lotrece watched the girl's eyes go sad with pity, and then child allowed mother to fall into her and Valencia became some type of comfort.

Mom, you'll have your plants and work and the gym and your book club and your girls' trips with the aunts. Don't be sad.

Please don't, she'd said, tapping her gently on the shoulder. And Lotrece had only nodded, knowing that a terrible end had come.

The three-hour ride back home that day was quiet and tone-setting. Clayton turned on sports talk radio and she closed her eyes and pretended to sleep. And that was the way things were from then on. They did their own things and avoided each other as best they could.

Lotrece thought about that as she made her way down the hallway. The floorboards squeaked beneath her feet, but she didn't worry about waking Clayton. He slept deep, even though he claimed not to. He did a lot of things and claimed he did not. The very thought of it made Lotrece grit her teeth.

She made her way through the darkness. She knew the house by heart. They'd lived there for ten years and she'd hated the place for nine. After a year as a homeowner with Clayton, she'd wanted to return to renting. She wanted to return to a place where things would be fixed without a fight. Where her home didn't feel like it was falling apart around her. But Clayton called her foolish for wanting such a thing. *You know how many black folk want to own they own anything?* he asked.

For nine years, she Gorilla Glued things to keep them running. The downstairs bathtub faucet, the overhead kitchen door cabinet, and the peeling tile in the master bathroom. She'd do a sloppy and pathetic job on purpose. She wanted Clayton to know that he was failing her. In most instances, she'd have asked him to fix things several times before resorting to her glue jobs. He'd often go on as if he didn't see the yellow glue puffing from its intended surface. He'd go on as if there had never been an issue at all.

When she knew she was near it, she felt for the light switch. The kitchen struggled to become illuminated, and she sighed at the final dimness it achieved. One of the fluorescent tubes had been out for months. It had been just as long since she'd cooked a good meal. Since she'd bared her teeth at her husband and said, *If you can't adhere to my honey-do list, I can't cook for you.* These days, when she was feeling most resentful toward him, she would fry one piece of fish or cook one slice of bacon and one egg and moan at the goodness loud enough for him to hear.

Clayton didn't seem to care, though. He loved food but seemed content with grabbing a burger or a pizza. She was the one who had a problem with that. She liked her meals prepared at home. She didn't need strangers touching, breathing, and passing gas all over and around food that she would consume. The thought of such things made her skin crawl.

But not Clayton. He didn't mind, nor did he seem to miss her cooking at all. He was a good cook himself. In the beginning of their marriage, he'd been a better one than her. He was creative in his approach and what he was willing to try. Her staple meals had always been similar to meals her mother made when she was a girl. Meatloaf and mashed potatoes, fried chicken or pork chops, spaghetti and corn, liver and onions, and pork-n-beans and weenies. Clayton would put on a crab boil in the middle of the week or pecan crusted trout on a Monday. He'd bypass catfish and deep-fry paiche. He was the one who introduced her to sushi. She hated admitting her love for it. She hated him knowing that he'd led her to it.

These days, though, their kitchen life had gone dim. He wouldn't dare walk into the kitchen and bend her over the sink like he used to. She knew it was in part because she couldn't hide her disgust for him. She also knew it had a lot to do with Angelica. And Kendra. And Veneshia.

The tile on the kitchen floor wasn't cold, but she stepped across it as if it was. She felt the thin coat of oil from his one-man oyster fry the night before under her feet. She considered going back into the bedroom and sliding into her slippers, but she dismissed the thought. It pissed her off that she even had to consider it. "Damn floor should be clean," she mumbled. She hated cleaning up after Clayton.

The whole time he stood in the kitchen the night before, she was angry. She stole glances at him from the pit group in the living room, where she'd sat watching reruns of *227*, *Amen*, and *Diff'rent Strokes* since she'd come in from work.

When he finally emerged from the kitchen and said, *I'm done. Some oysters in there if you want them*, she ignored him. Pretended that he wasn't even there. Kept her eyes on the television and acted as if he hadn't said a word. She felt him stand there for a while. She felt his face melt with pain and then she felt him walk away.

She smiled, pleasured by his pain, pleasured by her momentary victory. She turned her head to the spot he'd stood in and sighed. She thought about calling him back. Asking him if he'd had enough. If he had learned his lesson. If there would ever be another Angelica or Kendra or Veneshia. She knew better, though.

Clayton had always been easy to hurt, ever since they started dating in high school, but he didn't seem to be learning a thing from her lessons. Across all the years, he remained the same.

The paper-towel-lined glass bowl still sat on the island. She stepped close enough to look inside to see that the oysters were untouched. She exhaled. Clayton didn't eat oysters. Never had. But he knew that she loved a good fried piece of seafood on Friday evenings. When they were young, he loved joining her and her mother for Catfish Fridays. After they were married, he took Catfish Fridays on as his. She had hoped he'd thrown the oysters out after realizing that she had gone to bed without touching them. If he had done that, she would have been somewhat justified in her anger toward him. But the oysters sat there like kindness. She considered it cruel. Even after sitting uncovered in the darkness, the oysters looked delectable. The goldenness of the nuggets told her that he'd squirted them with spicy brown mustard before coating them with his special mixture of seasoned cornmeal and flour. He'd fried them to what he knew she considered perfection, and as badly as she wanted to reach out and grab a handful, she resisted. He needed to hurt more and know that she was master of her own heart. He didn't deserve the reward of her eating what he believed was prepared in love.

"Shit," she said, slapping her hand on the marble top of the island. "He always choosing the wrong damn thing."

Lotrece pushed herself away from the island and walked toward the refrigerator. When she opened it, she smiled at her own work. It was neatly organized, something she hadn't been able to achieve until the children were gone. She would often find ranch dressing, barbeque sauce, and ketchup containers or spills on the top shelf, which she felt should be strictly dedicated to beverages and such. Condiments were door items, but her children never seemed to catch on to that concept. She shuddered when she thought about the filth they likely lived in after they left home.

Even though she wasn't thirsty, she grabbed a water bottle from the top shelf, opened it, and took a sip. She closed the refrigerator, left the kitchen, and made her way back to the bedroom. She turned on the hall light and left it on for the sliver of light it provided and then stepped carefully to Clayton's side of the room.

His nightstand was still her nightstand and held all of her undergarments. They hadn't bothered to make the move official enough to change that. She didn't want him to wake with her standing above him naked, on his side of the bed. Though if he woke smiling, assuming she was inviting him into her after all this time, after ten months, she could take pleasure in letting him know that he was mistaken. She'd done enough with the oysters. Moderation was the key to getting him to understand the terms of their life together these days.

She squatted to pull the bottom drawer open, and when the wood scraped the side of the base, she paused and looked up at him. His snores had been soft, but they picked up, and he moved his leg and coughed. She stayed still by the nightstand until he settled. When she could measure the pauses between his snores, she pulled at the drawer again. From his side, the sliver of light was faint, so she simply stuck her hand in the drawer and felt around. She knew her panties by touch. The ones she loved were fairly old and worn and at the front of the drawer, but for some reason, she felt past them. She felt for the ones in back. The thongs and the lacey things that used to make Clayton look twice.

A sinister smile spread across her lips when she thought of his face if he woke up and found the covers kicked from her body. If he found her dressed in lacey underwear. She thought of the desire he would feel, but how he'd be quick to remember that she no longer let him touch her.

She was thinking of his hunger and her rejecting it when she felt it. Her smile slid away and she remembered the night at the old house. The night with the raccoons. It was the night their son forgot to close the top on the dog food tub and left the whole thing out on the screened porch. She remembered how she had let out a frightened scream when she turned on the light and peered out the door and found a family of raccoons feasting on the food. Clayton had run from their bedroom and stood behind her, clutching his robe, and she had smelled herself on his breath when he said, *What is it, baby? What's wrong?*

She'd remained silent, letting him figure it out by following her gaze. He stood there, and for a moment, she felt safe. And then she turned her eyes to his. They darted from raccoon to raccoon and she wondered what he was thinking. She stood there staring at him as his eyes almost bounced to the rhythm of the raccoons crunching on the other side of the door. He turned and walked away; she was surprised when he returned, carrying a small handgun, and gently pushed her aside.

He twisted the knob without actually opening the door before brandishing the gun at the animals. The biggest raccoon was the only one to look up from the tub.

Clayton tapped on the glass of the French door and yelled, "*You better get out of here!*"

The raccoon stared up at him, considering him for a while before finally signaling the rest of the gang of four to lift their heads from the tub. The leader raccoon led the others to where they had sliced their way through the screen, and it sat on one of the wooden beams that held the whole porch in place and sort of held the screen open as the gang filed out through the slit one at a time.

She often thought about the pounding in her chest that night. About switching that porch light on and seeing the raccoons' bladelike fingers, gripping the side of the tub. About how her first thought was of her mother and how she always felt safe with her. She even thought about that momentary safety she'd felt before she saw the fear in her husband's eyes, and she wondered what it all meant and why she could never let it go.

She didn't ask Clayton that night when or where he got the gun. She didn't ask him what he hoped to achieve by waving it at the animals. She let the whole ordeal rest when he opened his arms and told her, *Come on. Let's go back to bed.* She simply leaned into him, slept on his chest all night, and dreamt of herself with the gun. Only in her dream, instead of twisting the doorknob and letting it go, she opened it and shot the raccoons one by one.

They battled with the raccoons for two springs. The animals moved into the attic and then under the screened porch. Lotrece developed a personal vendetta against them, which led to a hate so fiery she had a hard time not bringing them up in any conversation she had. One of the other licensed vocational nurses at work bought her a book on raccoon mating for her birthday. She thought it an insult until the woman explained that Lotrece talked about them so much that she felt that deep down she had developed a sort of fascination with the animals. Lotrece trashed the book and stopped talking to the woman.

She finally succeeded in getting rid of the raccoons by poisoning them with ground round and huge amounts of d-Con. In the end, her only regret was that she had not achieved this before the numerous roof repairs and destroyed porch screens. She never told Clayton about the poison and he never seemed to notice they were gone. She always thought it was because that second spring was around the time he took up with Veneshia. But after she ruined the raccoons in that way, broke up their family with a good meal, she knew she could be cruel. She knew it was like art.

Now, in her panty drawer, she felt it under her fingertips and she remembered the raccoons. She knew what it was without the sliver of light from the hallway; she felt around it until she was gripping the handle. She knew it didn't work. That it hadn't worked since the day Clayton found it among his dead father's belongings, but it was something he'd held on to and she'd never questioned him about it after that first time. Days after the raccoons invaded the dog food, she asked him why he never told her about the gun. Where he kept it. He simply shrugged his shoulders and said, *It don't work. It broke a long time ago. Ain't no more dangerous than a toy gun. I keep it put up, though. Don't want the kids to get no ideas.*

After that, she hadn't felt the need to give him a gun safety or control talk. His words—*It don't work. It broke a long time ago*—established an assurance that the children were safe, and she had no intentions of touching it, so it seemed a harmless thing, his broken gun.

But there, with her hand gripped around the handle, it felt like an assault that he had placed it in the drawer with her undergarments. It seemed an infiltration, even, and she tried to figure out what it meant that he chose to place it there.

The second affair was with Kendra. After everything blew up, Lotrece promised him that there would be no more chances. Told him that she might kill him if it happened again. And then he scraped and saved, taking on more routes, sometimes driving goods all the way to Missouri, and treated her to seven days in Aruba. She fell for him all over again in a hammock on the beach. They were like newlyweds for almost five years, until the fibroids came along and caused all the trouble with her body. And then ten months ago, Angelica happened. Lotrece found her text messages in Clayton's phone. Images of her plump, naked body. *Call me when you can*, over and over. By that time, Lotrece was past forty. In her mind, the days of her youth were gone. She was too old to leave. Letty, a single coworker, told her, *Girl, ain't nobody checking for old women out here. You better stay where you at*, when she confided in her about possibly leaving her husband.

And so she stayed and punished him by not letting him touch her and pretending she hadn't stayed. But she hated that she could not keep her word and leave. She hated that he'd robbed her of her youth.

When she lifted the gun from the drawer, she realized that she'd somehow forgotten the heaviness of one. She stood and gripped it tightly in both hands, spreading her legs apart. She straightened her shoulders and thought about her mother teaching her to aim with confidence. She lifted the gun, pointing it in Clayton's direction.

She wondered what he'd think if he knew that she had followed him to Angelica's the night after she discovered the texts. That she circled the block when she saw him park in the driveway and had made it back around in time to see the thick Hispanic woman holding the screen door open with one extended arm and cradling a tabby cat in the other as he walked, almost skipped, to her. She wondered what they had been doing when she came back an hour later and his car was still there. Where they were when she took the d-Con and canned tuna from the grocery bag and boldly walked to the porch, hoping to find the cat's bowl.

There were times after that night that she wanted to ask him. She wanted to come right out and say, *Hey, whatever happened to Angelica's cat?* Most times, she hated him for bringing that out of her.

As she moved closer to her sleeping husband, she wasn't concerned about waking him up anymore. She inched the gun closer until the tip of the barrel was on his head. And she noticed when his snoring stopped and she could see the whites of his eyes spreading wide on his face. She stood with the gun gripped in her hands against his head, as he strained to focus his eyes. And she imagined it all coming together in his mind.

"Lotrece, baby?" he called out to her in a question. And he stuttered through asking her what was going on.

But he kept his body still underneath the weight of his father's gun. And she felt like a failure, like she was doing the right thing with the wrong thing because everything she did was either never enough or way too much. Because the gun didn't work.

When she loosened her grip on the gun, Clayton moved in one swift motion and clicked the switch on the nightstand lamp.

She stepped back, keeping the gun pointed in his direction. Her mother once told her, *If you ever pull a gun on a man, you better damn well mean it. You better blow his brains out right then and there.* She wondered if she'd pull the trigger if the gun were functional. She thought about what he'd mean to her dead.

Clayton let his back rest against the headboard and his eyes were wide and somewhat crossed as he tried to keep them on the hole of the barrel. He looked as if he was thinking something and Lotrece wondered what it was. Wondered what this all meant to him. He shifted his eyes to hers and then back to the gun. They began to dart widely, and that's when she saw it. The same thing she saw the night of the raccoons. It was something vulnerable. Something like fear.

After a while he shifted his gaze to the nightstand and sighed when he saw the open drawer. He exhaled and brought his hand to the top of his bald head, letting it slide down his face slowly, as if he was wiping something off. As if he was preparing for something.

He cleared his throat and told her to put the gun down. "I done tried everything I can to make it right with you, Lo," he said. "Put the goddamn gun down," he said, like he meant it. Like he wanted her to know he meant it.

She thought to ask him why she should put it down, but she knew by the fear in his eyes. She knew that it had all been a lie. From the very beginning. That night with raccoons. *It don't work. It broke a long time ago.* Him saying that he had not been physical with any of those women. The oysters on the island. They had all been lies. Something in her had always known. She wasn't, however, sure that he knew she knew.

"I should just pull the trigger," she said, taunting him, almost playfully.

"Don't play like that," he replied nervously. "E-even if it don't work, don't play," he said, like he really believed it. "Girl, you don't even pull no *broke* gun on a man."

"You think I can't, don't you?" They locked eyes. She saw him, so suave and handsome all those years ago. In his letterman jacket with his broad shoulders and godly perfection. Always saying the right thing. Doing the right thing to turn her on. She wondered if she *could* do it. If she could shoot *that* man. If she could pull the trigger and stop his life and change the rest of hers. She thought of suppressing her anger and warring subtly and she thought of making him pay for everything.

"You think I can't, don't you?" she asked again, but this time the question was more to herself.

And she thought of her children in the house with this gun all those years. She thought of Clayton's easy lies, and how she tried to understand him, believe him through them.

And for the first time since she'd found those text messages in his phone, she felt tears coming from the center of her and she knew she could do it. She could kill this man who had once been a dream of hers. She could and she would and knowing that they had reached that point broke something in her.

She was the first to break their stare. She shook her head like he was something pathetic. Something unworthy. And he sat there trembling.

She lowered the gun gently—carefully—and placed it on the nightstand before she turned her back to walk away.

"You lucky it's, what you say, *broke*," she scoffed.

When she made her way out of the bedroom, she made sure to sway her hips in a way that he would never forget. When she looked over her shoulder to see if the man she once loved was watching, his eyes were closed and his head lay against the headboard. His shoulders rose and fell quickly with each deep breath he took in and released.

She smiled at that. It didn't matter that he wouldn't remember the sway of her hips. His fear in that moment gave her the first delight she'd felt in a long while.

PATERNAL

....

For her

He ain't ask to be here, so I tried to love him as much as I could. Sometimes, though, when I looked at him, all I could see was you. Same deep curly hair, puffy lips, and droopy eyes. But he had some of me too. Like his forehead was too long and all his fingers looked like thumbs. And sometimes, when he opened his eyes, I could see he was lost and alone in the world. All he needed was to be loved. All he wanted was that. That part there was me.

And I was trying to get my life back on track from where fooling around with you knocked it off-balance. I can't even remember what made me look at you in the halls of that high school in the first place. Whatever it was is exactly what had me sitting in the WIC office the first time the stripper you took up with called me a bitch. Sitting up there waiting for them to give me the vouchers that give me the milk to feed your child. A child I was having a hard time looking at. A child I didn't want in the first place.

The lady that sat beside me had her man with her. She was from the Middle East, I guess. Had her head all covered up and kept her eyes down on her baby. She was just there for stuff like cheese and beans and peanut butter. I know cause at one point she took the baby under her clothes. Whole baby disappeared. I knew she was breastfeeding. Everybody in the waiting room did. Still, her man stood in front of her the whole time the baby was under her clothes. Guess he was trying to block us from seeing her. Trying to protect her from our eyes.

If I hadn't met you, I wouldn't have been sitting there. If you had been the type of father you promised to be, maybe that would've been you protecting me. Or maybe you would've been buying your son's milk altogether. I wouldn't have had to beg nobody's government agency cause you sell enough drugs to take care of your own child.

By then, I'd heard you liked to spray the strip club with money and that you bought a new motorcycle. Heard you and that stripper rode together on Saturday nights, moved in together, and was real serious about each other. Heard you was doing real good for yourself.

And I was just sitting there listening to the chatter around me when somebody somewhere behind me with a voice that was both familiar and unfamiliar started talking.

"Girl, that nigga is a straight-up trick," the voice said. Then I heard giggling. "Bet I won't complain about it. I'm just trying to do me."

It only took a few seconds for me to know, but after them seconds, I knew it was her. I wanted to turn and see. Get a good look at her face, but I didn't want trouble. It sounded like the same voice that answered your phone when I called to tell you I was in labor. That's when I first found out about her. I thought we were still together until she told me different. After that, she handed the phone to you. Told you to tell me and you got on the line and said it was over. I shouldn't call again; you had moved on. After that, I wasn't nothing no more.

I didn't have to turn around. After a while I heard her say, "That look like his ex-bitch up there." She sucked her teeth and said, "Just stupid. Sitting in here looking for a handout and he giving everything he got to me."

I didn't turn around. I made like I ain't hear nothing. But if the folks around me would've looked close enough, they would've seen my whole body shaking. I couldn't control it. Couldn't make it stop. I wasn't scared or nothing like that. I'm not sure exactly what the emotion was. I guess it was the kind of shaking that come when a person know something major just changed in they life. Know they got to decide and it's all on them. I just sat there, shaking and holding my bag close to my chest, waiting for my number to be called. Waiting for my turn.

When he was three months old, the baby got sick. I admit I had slipped into the habit of calling you and saying stuff going on with him sometimes just to hear your voice. Let you hear mine. I thought maybe if you heard me, you'd remember we had a child together and I was once worth something to you. Maybe if I pronounced all my words right and sounded like I was doing better for myself, you'd remember what we used to have and want to get it back.

But when the baby got sick, I wasn't just looking to hear your voice or nothing like that. I really needed money for medicine and some support outside of what my momma and her husband gave. I was at a point to where I was tired of seeing them struggle to help me and your baby not struggle.

When I called you at midnight, the stripper answered and said, "Bitch, stop calling my man this late. He don't want your dumb ass no more." She hung up laughing and I imagined you laughing beside her.

My momma tried to tell me that hanging out with people from your neighborhood was gone get me in trouble, but I was sixteen. Your sister and cousins were nice to me. Asked me for rides everywhere. Welcomed me into y'all world and it felt good to be part of something. Something that wasn't square or Christian, like the nerdy dudes that approached me or the church boys my momma approved of.

She would say stuff like, *I don't want you to be like me. Why you think we work so hard?* When I'd get caught on *your* side of town, she'd say, *We struggle to pay for this big old house out here with these white folks. We struggle so you can do better. Make better choices than what we made.* I always rolled my eyes at her words when she wasn't looking.

I couldn't see how or where my momma and her husband struggled. Our lights always came on when I flicked the switch. We always had food and they were able to buy me nice clothes and things when I asked for them. Y'all were constantly being sat out of houses and apartments, going without food, and even living with friends and relatives. I felt for y'all and resented my parents and maybe myself for having what y'all didn't.

I was eighteen when your stripper cussed me out and hung up on me like that. After she was off my line, I sat there looking down at the warm baby in my arms and thought about the acceptance letter I got from that university in Kentucky the year before. I wished I could go back to that choice. I wished I had the opportunity to laugh in your face when you made your voice all sweet and asked me to keep your child. I told myself if I could do it all over, I'd choose well. I'd get it right.

My momma lost her job at Blockbuster Distribution Center a few months after I got pregnant. They laid almost everybody off. The demand for VHS cassettes and even DVDs was way down. We struggled for months on just her husband's income before they lost the house and we had to rent a smaller place.

All that time we was struggling, I knew I made the wrong decision when I kept your baby. When I first found out I was pregnant, I had Kentucky on my mind and wasn't thinking about having nobody's kid. I told you that. Asked you to go half with me on the procedure, but you and your sweet tongue talked me into keeping it. Told me we'd raise it together. Be a family. You even cried real tears and said you couldn't bear not being there for your kid. You couldn't bear being like your father. I saw them tears and let go of all of the dreams my momma must've been holding on to for me. If she had told me—been honest with me long before the day she lost her job—that we had always just been barely holding on, maybe things would've turned out different.

When she came into my room, wearing her headscarf and gown, and sat on the bed beside me, after your stripper hung up on me, when she touched your baby's forehead with the back of her hand, when she smacked her lips and sighed, I felt guilty. When she asked, "What that nigger say?" I saw the tired in her eyes and heard the disappointment in her voice. I wanted to take it all back. I wanted to take every time I snuck out with you back. Finding out I was pregnant and listening to you and not telling her and forgetting my future. I wanted to take it all back and make things right with her again.

She put her hand on my shoulder and shook her head. "Give him here. I'll take him," she said, reaching her arms out to take your son from my arms. "You get some sleep, baby. I got him."

I carefully passed your baby over to her and she positioned him in her arms, gently tapped his little bottom, and said, "Granny's little man gone be just fine."

A few months later, your sister called and cussed me out. Something about bringing drama to you and your girlfriend and my baby not being yours. I hung up on her. I was doing okay without help from you, and me and my momma and her husband was making strides with all of us working and taking turns looking after your child.

He was a sickly little thing, real prone to colds and stuff, but we had all come to depend on his smiles and coos to keep us in the family room at night. He'd brought us together in a way I thought was destroyed when I was sixteen. When I was with you.

The night your sister called, we was sitting in the front room watching a horror movie. My momma's husband had got off work early, so he had been the one to pick the baby up from the sitter, who told him the baby wasn't feeling well. Said we should monitor him closely. So we was all kind of positioned in front of the TV around him, like he was Jesus in the manger. Every time he kicked and cooed, we laughed and commented on how precious he was.

When my momma asked me who was on the phone, I lied and said, "Wrong number." But when it rang again and she picked it up, she found out for herself.

"Look here," she said, making her face all firm and serious. "My girl don't ask y'all for nothing. Y'all ain't got nothing. Don't call my house no more with that. You do, you gone have to deal with me," she said, and then she hung up on your sister. The phone didn't ring again that night. We just sat there and watched the movie and every now and then we smiled at our messiah and the whole time you and your family was somewhere hating me for something I never did. The whole time we sat there smiling at your son, I was thinking about that.

I was at work and the baby was with my momma when my boss called me to the phone with a irritated look on his face. He shoved the receiver in my direction, leaned in close, and whispered, "No personal calls. This is a place of business."

His pinched, red face looking down at me made me feel small and like I could lose everything on count of a phone call. Up to that point, I had never received a call at work. I hardly received calls at home.

As soon as I placed the phone to my ear and said hello, Momma said, "The baby stopped breathing," sounding all out of breath herself. "We called the ambulance. Meet us at the hospital."

I was real close to asking her how I was gone get there. They had lost my car a few months before I had the baby. And then I remembered I had theirs. I remembered that we was sharing everything. Car. Baby. Just everything. Momma sounded nervous, like she really believed the baby stopped breathing, even though I didn't. Even though I knew she had made a mistake. But because we was so close and sharing and understanding, I needed to share this with her too. So I said, "Yes, ma'am. I'm on my way."

As I made my way to the hospital, I thought about calling you, but you hadn't seen the baby once since he was born. Hadn't had nothing to do with us. My calls to you had pretty much stopped, and my family had turned into what you was supposed to be.

At the hospital, they checked the baby out, said he was okay but they would keep him overnight for observation. Like me, they doubted he'd stopped breathing. I'm sure in they eyes, my momma was a black woman who ain't know nothing about life or breathing. Momma and her husband went home and I settled into a room with the giant baby bed pushed in beside a small bare cot for me. The baby had been quiet through all the testing, like he was too over things to cry. Looking at him hooked up to all the tubes and machines kind of scared me and made me feel like even though they said he was fine, he was slipping away.

I stared at the bedside phone for as long as I could, and then I dialed your number. To my surprise, you answered it yourself and it took me a long time to register that I wasn't being cussed out and to say something back to your repeated hellos.

I stuttered out your name, like a question.

You said *yeah*, like you was expecting something else.

I hurried and told you about the baby and the hospital, even about him not breathing. I pushed all them words out, hoping you wouldn't hang up on me. Hoping you'd hear me out and maybe come for the child *you* wanted.

You cussed. Said, *Shit, man*. And asked me why I didn't call earlier, like I should've known it was okay to do that, like I hadn't ever tried. You reminded me that it was your birthday. Told me you had plans. And I was sorry about interrupting your life with such a minor thing. When I was fixing my mouth to say those words, you asked which hospital. Said you might stop by later.

Something inside me leapt, like unexpected hope. I gave you the information, happy that you answered and not your stripper. Happy you was even willing to stop by and see about your son. Right before the phone clicked, I called out your name. I didn't wait for you to answer before I told you happy birthday. I don't think you heard me, though. I think you was already gone.

After that, I sat on the cot while the baby slept peacefully in the bed beside me and thought about my momma and her husband having a free night. How much they deserved it on the count of what they'd been to us those past six months. I thought about you coming and seeing you got a family and maybe being sorry you done missed so much of it. I thought about Kentucky and for the first time I didn't think about what your son caused me to miss. I thought about how Kentucky was still there. How I could still go and make that right for my momma. I thought about taking your son with me. About taking you with us.

And I thought about all my regret and all my tears over those months, and I decided to be what I needed to be for him. I wanted to whisper these things to him. To tell him these things and kiss him and be a mother to him. I wanted to tell him we was gone be all right. The three of us. That we was gone be a family and he was gone be raised up right.

I stood up and took the one step toward his bed and looked down at his sleeping form. I could feel the tears in my eyes for all the thoughts I'd had about him. For all the times I'd blamed him and regretted not having that procedure. For all the times I didn't want him to be my son.

And then his little body started vibrating and shaking like he was a laughing doll just put down, like my thoughts and my intentions was the funniest thing in the world. But he also looked scared and like he needed me to do something or to stop doing something, so I looked down at the floor to make sure I hadn't stepped on nothing. When the room started beeping like everything was falling apart, I got scared.

A nurse came through the door and I tried to tell her he was in trouble, and she pulled my arm out the door as a flood of other folks rushed in. She put me in a small room with a table and chairs and told me I should call my momma. That I should call someone. I looked at the phone on the table. I thought about you and your sister and the stripper. I thought about my momma and her husband.

When my momma and her husband arrived, still wearing their pajamas, I felt like I had been in the little room for hours.

"What happened? What they say, baby?" Momma said.

"They said they trying," I said, and I felt like I was in a dream, in a daze.

There was a knock on the door and a doctor walked in. He was white, bald, and nervous.

"Please," he said, stretching his arms out toward the seats. My momma looked down at them and gently pushed me to sit down, but her husband told the doctor he would rather stand.

"Very well," the doctor said. "We tried very hard. We did everything we could, but we couldn't save him."

My momma's face slid down into a frown and she asked, "Save him from what? What you mean?"

"I'm sorry. We did everything we could," the doctor said, standing there looking at us like we was all something pitiful before he finally dropped his head and turned to leave us in the little room.

My momma started crying and her husband caught her falling body. I sat in the chair, repeating, "We couldn't save him," over and over again. No matter how many times I said it, I couldn't make it right in my head. Right in my heart. I kept wondering if my son knew I loved him. If I ever really learned to before that moment. So many memories crashed into me as I tried to figure it out. Pushing him out. Being stitched up after. Trying to get him to latch onto my nipples. My first night at home with him. His screeching cry. His soiled diapers. When he first opened those droopy eyes and looked at me. The time he peed in my face and seemed amused by it. How I learned to dodge his little shooter. His first smile. The first time he intentionally placed his soft hand on my cheek. The secondhand-store crib he wouldn't sleep in. Him hogging the twin bed that had once been only mine. Me wrapping my arms around him and cradling him through the night. Me pressing my nose into that sweet-baby-mixed-with-puke smell that belonged to me and him. Him reaching for me when I came in from work. The brown sugar teddy bear I planned to buy him when I got my next paycheck.

And I didn't think of you at all.

In the end, after we'd made the arrangements to have him taken to the funeral home, after we'd cried over his lifeless body, after we'd let the loss set in, my momma's husband comforted both of us. He held each of us in his arms, guided us out of the hospital, where we were met by the gloomy morning sky, into the parking lot, where you were just arriving.

It was the first time I'd seen you since before the baby was born. You were dressed like you'd been to a club, like you'd been celebrating your birthday, like you didn't have a son. When you saw us, you smiled and walked over to where my momma's husband was putting her in the car.

Where y'all going? Where my son at, man? you asked, smiling, showing a completely gold set of teeth. It was a new thing. You didn't have gold teeth the last time I saw you. They made you look like somebody else. Something else. You no longer looked like the boy I fell for. The boy with spacey teeth that protruded slightly in the front, revealing a gap. In that moment, as you stood there with questions in your eyes, you looked like a rapper. Or a drug dealer. Or a murderer.

In that moment, I hated your deep curly hair, puffy lips, and droopy eyes. And that's why, after he made sure she was situated in the car, I let my momma's husband guide me into the car without acknowledging you at all.

You stood there watching us leave the hospital without your son. Without my son. As we pulled out of the parking space and you peered through the window into my eyes, I think you knew and I think you didn't.

EVERYTHING'S FINE

Listen. I ain't got but about fifteen minutes to tell you this stuff. Got be back inside that building cause my break'll be up. Lunch and breaks, I take in my car. The only way to escape the stink of death that's waiting for me inside. So I'm gone need you to listen good.

Everything I do, I do under the direction of the heavenly father himself. Shoot, that's what make things easier for me. The fifth chapter of Galatians say if you be led by the spirit then you ain't bound by the law. I believe that more than I believe what I see when I stand in the mirror.

Everything I do, I do for God. That mean everything I do, I do for you too. So I guess it's only right I be honest with you. Been feeling different here lately. When I look at you . . . I don't know. Things just ain't the same. I member us being young and in school. In love. You in that rich girl school. Me in the hood. You was so pretty and bright. Had the whole world in front of you. Wanted to fix broken children. Had a smile that shined up the whole city. I could see your smile from where I lived all the way on the other side of town. And woman, you was fine. I mean, real easy on the eyes. Them high cheekbones and tight eyes had all us going wild, but you chose me.

Don't take this the wrong way, Resh, but these days you ain't so easy to look at. Ain't got none of the dreams you had no more. You done let yourself go in so many ways. Give birth to Emagine three years ago and still ain't got back to yourself. Sit around all day, fussing at the kids and watching soap operas. Done gained eighty pounds just sitting there. Sometimes I wonder if you ever even open that study Bible I bought you. It ain't dog-eared, wrinkled up, or marked up like you do when you reading.

Foster kids, foster kids, foster kids. Always hassling me about foster kids. Can't believe you ain't happy with my uncle getting me this slaughterhouse job. It's a good job to get in this town. Cost of living ain't as high as it was when we in Austin. We can get back up on out feet without getting more fosters since I'm working. Can't you see that, darling? Ain't that good enough for you?

I tried being quiet as I could this morning when I was getting ready for work. I didn't want to wake you up. Tiptoed round that room. That room we sometimes share with one of our fosters—sometimes both of our fosters and our real daughter too. This morning they was all in there with us. The girls come in from the room they share down the hall last night. They was scared, I guess. Kids get scared sometimes, but I ain't got to tell you that. That's your ministry, Resh. Kids. I just need you to get back to remembering that.

You ain't been happy with me since we moved in your momma's rent house. It's been months since you really looked at me. And I don't understand it. This a nice house. Nicer than anything I ever lived in when I was growing up. Got high ceilings, marble floors, cherubs painted above the entryways, and even a second floor. Don't bother me none. Living in it. I thought it a blessing when your momma told us we ain't have to pay her no rent. Just keep up the utilities and cable if we want it.

And I just ain't want to hear your mouth this morning. Always with the fosters. Fosters, fosters, fosters.

You need to call Velma down at the agency on your break, you said, from the darkness. You ain't whisper like somebody who ain't want wake the kids, and your voice wasn't groggy like you had really been sleeping. I freezed up, like I was in a trap or something. I couldn't reply to you, Resh. Wanted you to go back to sleep. When I ain't say nothing, you did. *I want to get out of Mother's house sometime this year.*

Resh, I said, and I know you could hear that I was nervous in my voice. I hate being on your bad side. I want you to love me. Just want to make you happy. *I—I just started working and membership at the church is climbing. Baby, give me—*

I don't want to hear it, you hissed at me, like a cottonmouth ready to strike. Then I heard a soft, steady thump from the same darkness your voice come from. I knew you was patting the baby, Jackson, back. He must've stirred in his sleep. You wasn't ready to get up and make his bottle. You never ready to make his bottle or do anything else for him. I like Jackson, though. He got a old man smile. Make him seem wiser than his nine months. Shoot, make him seem wiser than my twenty-nine years.

I don't have time to wait on you to save enough money from a slaughterhouse job. I sure as hell don't have time to be waiting on your members. They have even less than us, Ben. Call the woman.

I couldn't help but think of Apostle Paul. He gave us fair warning against this marriage business. He said he who is married has to care for the things of this world. Amen? If I ain't spend all my time trying make you happy, ain't no telling what I could be doing for the Lord.

I ran my hand across the old chest-dresser, feeling for my keys. The kids' snoring was nice to my ears, but I could still hear your angry breathing over them. You always mad at me these days. Want me to say something about you never cooking or cleaning. Want me to cuss and fuss, I guess. Maybe you just want a reason to get rid of me. I don't know what's going on with you, Resh, but I'm patient. God make folks just the way he want them. I'm posed to love you like Christ loves the church. We ain't all together right, is we? And he wait on us. Amen?

You and me . . . we still young. I figure we can find our way back to the loving once we get past all these money problems.

I'm gone be late tonight. Got to stop and check on Sister Price. Pray for her mother, I said, when I felt the cold keys under my hand.

You voice was softer when you spoke again: *Just be sure to call Velma, Ben. Call me and let me know what she says.*

Jackson was sucking hard on his pacifier. It keep him quiet when nothing else can. Every now and then, he let out a baby moan that made me want to smile. I always wanted a son, but you keep reminding me that Jackson ain't it.

That way, I can get that room down the hall cleaned up. Just in case she wants to come by and see it, you said.

I nodded my head up and down at you, but you couldn't see me. I knew that. I was glad you couldn't. You would've seen my disappointment in what you becoming.

Resh, God ain't forgot us. We just got to keep standing on his word. Doing what's right, I said to you.

You sighed, irritated with me. *Just call the agency, Ben.*

Now I'm sitting in this car. Last break of the day and I still ain't called Velma. I ain't calling her either. You ain't got enough love for the two fosters we got. You want another for the wrong reason. God will provide. We can't be using his children. These babies' lives been hard enough. Poor Jackson. Found shaking in a dumpster. Ain't nobody want him cause he born on drugs. We was in a bind when Velma called us with him. Broke. Not a dime to our names. Hadn't been for that, you wouldn't have wanted him either.

I'm the husband and God done give me dominion over our house. Over you. I might be struggling as a provider right now, but you gone get in line behind me cause I'm standing behind God. I want you to see this in my eyes, Resh. See it the way I slump my shoulders when I'm with you. Do you want to lose me? Do you?

. . .

The longer Resha sat on the couch, the more her frustration grew. After Ben's phone call, she was numb. Then Jackson started screaming to the top of his lungs from the upstairs bedroom. He carried on for more than an hour. She knew he was just a baby, but he was getting under her skin. She couldn't hear how Rex and Celeste's reconciliation talk was going. She'd waited all morning to watch *Days of Hope*, her favorite soap opera, and now she couldn't even hear it. She'd just popped the last chocolate-covered almond from her weekly two-pound bag into her mouth, which meant she was out of her favorite snack, and this only added to her irritation. She let out a loud growl and stood up from her sunken spot on the couch. She frowned when she felt something squish between her toes. She didn't have to look down past the big muumuu she was wearing to know that she had just stepped on the Play-Doh castle her three-year-old daughter and four-year-old foster child had made earlier.

"Emagine and Lucy," she called out. "Get your asses in here. Now." She stood still, keeping her foot on top of the dough until the girls came running to the family room. They still wore their pajamas. Emagine's hair was standing straight up on top of her head, which reminded Resha that, even uncombed, Lucy's hair looked better. Lucy's biracial features included green eyes and fine hair that wouldn't stand up on her head if she wanted it to. Resha couldn't deny that Lucy's features were agreeable. She resented the child for that. She'd prayed to the god her husband served to bless her own daughter with light skin and good hair. She didn't get that.

"What's under my goddamn foot?" she asked, pointing her finger at the floor and glaring at the girls through squinted eyes.

"Play-Doh," Emagine answered after Lucy didn't speak up.

"I was talking to her," Resha said, pointing at Lucy. "Answer me, little girl. I'm not playing with you."

Lucy's eyes watered over with tears and her lips began to quiver. "Emagine and me was playing with it."

Resha had never touched her out of anger or love, but Lucy was still terrified of her. Her eyes and the tone of voice let the little girl know she wasn't fond of her. She had been with them for a little over a year, and if it wasn't for the check every month, Resha would have given her back by now. Since Austin, her failed education, and what she called The Return, Resha had convinced herself she didn't like children. She even went as far as wondering why she had actually gone through her own pregnancy and given birth to Emagine.

"Get this shit up. Now," she said, through clinched teeth.

"I'll help, Mommy," Emagine said, dropping down to her knees.

Resha stepped around the children and made her way out of the living room. Being back in the small town depressed her. After high school, she married Ben and they left for Austin the same week. She thought she would never have to see tumbleweeds and dust storms again. Coming back to the home of her latter adolescent years had broken her.

When she was young, before Ben, she'd wished her mother had found her final husband in Chicago or New York, where they'd all have been happy. But Wiley Johnson had been from West Texas, where his family owned and operated a lucrative chain of funeral homes. Her mother hadn't hesitated to pack up their Atlanta apartment and leave the city to marry the cowboy boot–wearing, heavy, Southern-drawl-speaking man. Wiley was good to them, but his kindness never made up for the dusty town.

Things started out well in Austin. Ben played defensive lineman on a full scholarship at UT for a few years, and then dropped out to work while Resha continued her studies. He had some elaborate plan about sitting out of school a year and beginning the NFL walk-on tryout process. Resha didn't quite understand the process and wondered why he didn't just wait to be drafted after graduation, but when he explained to her that every black kid from a poor neighborhood was waiting on the same draft, she supported him. He tried out for Miami as a walk-on and was offered his chance. He forgot about college forever that day. A college education had never been his goal. It had always been football.

They made Austin their home base so that Resha could finish school, and Ben rented a condo in Miami. Resha didn't mind his constant absence because he provided her with all the things she thought she deserved. Then halfway through his rookie year, the seizures started. Even after that, when he lost his football contract, Resha thought they'd make it in Austin.

They formulated a new plan and decided that he would use the rest of his NFL funds to invest in his own business and she would finish school. After she completed her education, she planned to help her husband run his business and their home. In her mind, he deserved it. Her help and anything else she could give. He had overcome insurmountable odds, and she loved that he was worth so much more than his "black side" of town. But the emptiness that followed his broken football career led him to drinking and gambling. And then came Emagine.

Resha wanted to love her daughter and foster children, but anger somehow stopped her from doing so. She blamed Emagine for crushing her dream of becoming an adolescent therapist, and she blamed Ben for being weak—for being broken and for wanting to keep the baby. Sometimes she thought if Emagine hadn't been born, if she had been able to complete that final year, she could love children. But the child had been conceived at the worst possible time. Ben was at the height of his addiction and had gambled away all their money and their home. They were struggling to feed just the two of them. There was no way they could feed a baby and handle all the bills too. But Ben refused to agree to an abortion. He cried and found Jesus with the news of her pregnancy. Said God wasn't known for making mistakes; he was known for being perfect. Claimed God had revealed a new plan to him.

That was back when she loved Ben, so she forgave him and followed his revised plan. He was the only man she'd ever loved. But their life together wasn't supposed to be what it had become.

When she approached the staircase, Jackson's screams became soft cries. He was tired and sniffling, trying hard to catch his breath.

"Good," she said out loud. "Maybe he'll take his hollering ass to sleep."

She grabbed the rail with her hand and felt like crying when she saw her unkempt nails. Her mother hadn't raised her that way. She found out early on that towns in West Texas never integrated. She was far removed from where most blacks lived, so she was accustomed to luxuries that Ben didn't see as necessary in their times of struggle. When she was a girl, she attended private schools, sat for weekly hair appointments, and even visited France with her mother one summer. He had no idea how much her hands meant to her.

As she lifted her heavy foot up to the first step, she sighed and recalled her mother's warning after the first time she met Ben. *Girl, if you never listen to me again, listen good now*, she said. She was getting ready for a date with her husband. As Resha watched, she couldn't help but think that she was always getting ready for a date or a marriage to someone. As she applied her expensive makeup, Resha watched her from the long mirror in her oversized bathroom. She didn't respect her mother back then. She thought she was a self-hating, gold-digging hypocrite. She had made it out of the ghetto and wanted to pretend that she had never been there.

When she was young, Resha *thought* she wanted to rescue the black community. Her mother couldn't keep her out of Ben's neighborhood. She loved feeling close to "her people." Fortunately for Resha, her mother's house, the house she lived in now, was not in the black neighborhood. However, the church her husband pastored was, and it served as a constant reminder to her that as long as she was with Ben, she was just like the people in the black neighborhood. Poor.

She remembered her mother's warning that night. *Leave those boys from that ghetto alone, dear. They will pull you down to the same gutter they come from.* And then she rubbed her lips together to distribute the lipstick between her upper and lower lip. *He's a nice boy, Aresha. I'm not saying he's not. He's just not good enough for you, honey.*

And now she understood.

She couldn't hear Jackson crying anymore. He had tired himself out. She didn't worry about him falling off the bed. He had done that before, and it seemed he'd learned his lesson. No matter how long she left him in the bedroom screaming to the top of his lungs, he never moved from the center of the bed.

She made her way up to the top of the stairs and felt the sting of tears in her eyes. She worked out every day before Emagine. Her body had been beautiful. She was proud when she looked in the mirror and saw the ripples in her stomach and the firmness of every curve. Now she couldn't even climb a flight of stairs without wanting to pass out, and she certainly couldn't bear to look in the mirror at the stretch marks that resembled road maps and the dents all over her body.

She stopped and stared at the photo that sat on her mother's fancy wall-table at the top of the stairs. Life had been easy when the picture was taken. Her sister, Crissy, smiled back at her from inside the picture, and her brother, Stan, waved a peace sign. They were both climbing aboard a boat in Hawaii, a vacation their family took regularly in Resha's youth. Resha stood next to her mother on the deck of the boat looking down at her siblings. She remembered how wide her smile spread across her face that day.

She had been free under her mother's care, and even though she couldn't remember which of her mother's late husbands had taken the photo, she remembered her mother's ability to provide them with everything their young hearts desired.

The sound of the ringing phone jolted her from the daydream and apparently shook Jackson from his sleep. She knew it was Ben again. How dare he call back? Resha rolled her eyes to the low rumbling coming from Jackson, which signaled to her the beginning of his cry. She rushed to the room where he was and grabbed the cordless phone off the cradle before plopping down onto the bed next to him and patting him rapidly on his back. Sometimes it was easy to put him back to sleep. Other times her patting didn't work. She let out a sigh of relief when she noticed his eyes were still closed as he turned his little head from side to side, searching for his pacifier with his mouth. He slid his tiny lips around his only comfort until his lips connected with the nipple.

She hit the talk button and answered the phone with a soft "Hello."

"Aresha?" It was her mother's voice. Had she been more worried about waking Jackson, she would have gone to another room to answer the phone, one with a caller ID. She could have let it ring. *I can't stand that baby*, she thought as she looked down at his sleeping form.

"Hi, Mother," she said in an unenthused tone. "How are things in Florida?"

"I tried calling you twice earlier," her mother said without answering her question. "Is everything okay? Crissy said she tried calling too—"

"Everything's fine, Mother." Resha exhaled. "Things are actually good. Looks like we'll be moving out of your place soon—"

"Oh, never you mind that," her mother said with a chuckle. "That's not why I'm calling. I'll be there next week," she said with excitement. "Wiley has some business at the funeral home and I thought maybe—"

"Next week? You're coming back next week?" Resha's eyes darted around the room. It was a mess and she knew her mother's criticism would be unending if she saw the house that way. She had planned to do a thorough cleaning before her mother's return in April, but a week was hardly enough time. Ben cleaned a little here and there, but he spent most of his time off from work playing with the kids or at the church.

"But it's January, Mother. I thought you hated the unpredictability of Texas weather in the winter."

"Nonsense. A few days of that place won't hurt me. Plus, I want to see my Emagine . . . And your sister said she'd drive in from Dallas. A mini family reunion."

Resha couldn't find the right words to tell her mother that she didn't want her to come and visit her own home. She touched her uncombed hair and thought about what her mother would say if she saw it and the oversized muumuu she was wearing.

"Where is that husband of yours?" her mother asked.

"He's at work."

"At that church?" Her mother's tone was curious, and it irritated Resha.

"He was hired for a real job, Mother. Like I said, things are going great." Resha's tone was flat. She dreaded the question she knew her mother was about to ask.

"Really? Good for him." She sounded sincere enough to Resha, but she knew her mother too well. She had never supported her decision to marry Ben. She had even urged her to leave him after Emagine was born. She had been disappointed with Resha since she started dating "below her class" in high school. In her mother's eyes, she deserved what Ben was giving her. She deserved unhappiness. "Where at?" her mother asked.

Resha didn't want her to know her husband was laboring at a slaughterhouse. Both Crissy and her husband worked as attorneys in Dallas. Even her brother had made good. He was a podiatrist and lived far away from West Texas. She was the only one who hadn't done anything with her life. She didn't have a job or a complete education, and what Ben did didn't even count as work.

She grabbed as much as she could of the chunky flesh on Jackson's leg, between the knuckle of her index finger and her thumb, and twisted as hard as she could. Almost instantly, he spat the pacifier out of his mouth and a loud scream erupted.

"It's okay, Jack," she cooed at him sweetly as he tried to pull himself to his knees and crawl away from her. "Mother, I have to go," she said into the phone. "Jack is up from his nap."

"A-Aresha," her mother stuttered. "I am so proud of what you do for those children. It was always what you wanted. To work with children," she blurted out. There was a pause and then a short, "Um." It was as if she wanted to say more, but then she just hung up.

"Hush, boy," Resha commanded, patting the still screaming child on his back. She reached out and stuck the pacifier back into his mouth, and he began sucking but continued his fussy moans until he dozed back off to sleep.

"Sorry, Jack-Jack," she whispered, leaning in close enough to kiss the top of his soft head. "I didn't mean to hurt you. That was wrong. I just . . ."

She rubbed her hand across the fine hairs on the side of his head. He was calm now. Sleeping peacefully. She remembered when she loved children. Working to build them, the broken ones, into strong adults was all she ever wanted. She wanted to love Jackson and Lucy. She wanted to love Emagine with all her heart, but something was stopping her from doing it, and she didn't know how to fight it. Ben was always talking about prayer, but it hadn't helped her much when she tried it. Maybe it was him. Maybe his prayers and the passive way he chose to climb toward the success they deserved—she deserved. Maybe Ben was the problem. Who was she kidding? Ben *was* stopping her.

She stood up from the bed and placed the phone back on the

cradle. Passing the dresser, she paused at her own reflection in the mirror. She was unkept. Her hair was a mess and so was her body. She looked down at the muumuu she was wearing, letting her eyes glide down to her feet. Her toes, peeking from under the cloth, looked swollen they were so plump, and they made her remember her hard work at the gym so many years ago. She raised her hands and examined her palms as if she had never seen them before.

Her mother's phone calls were usually the most upsetting, but Ben's words had beat her mother to the punch today. Who did he think he was to command anything of her? To threaten her with his absence when she had been there for him through it all? To leave her in this state? He loved her. Once. She'd loved him, like there was no one else in the world. Enough to defy her mother. Enough to come back to the dirt. And he would leave her like this.

She smoothed her hands against her muumuu and raised her chin. She blinked away the tears from her eyes and peered at her face. She didn't recognize herself. The dark rings around her eyes made her look tired or sick, and the clusters of white bumps on her forehead turned her stomach. Makeup couldn't cover the ruin of her life. She would never be beautiful again, but Ben could not leave her.

She would not allow it. She would make him pay for his threat. She would submit. Let him think himself victorious. But he would be wrong in the end, and he would know it. She looked back at Jackson. Poor thing didn't stand a chance in the world. No matter what they did, they wouldn't save him. Ben's god would never tell them that truth. Everything was stacked against him from day one. All of them. Lucy. Emagine. And it was stacked against her from the moment she chose Ben. She would try again when Jackson was awake. She would love him and give him ice cream. She would bounce him on her knee the way Ben did. He seemed to like that quite a bit. She would apologize to the girls and look at them and love them. She would comb their hair and make them pretty. She would be happy and smile and dance with them.

She turned back to the dresser, where papers, mostly bills, were strewn about carelessly. She allowed her eyes to scan the clutter until she found what she was looking for, the keys to the old Monte Carlo. Ben bought the lemon when they were both still students at UT and it had never run consistently for more than a few months, so they gave it up to the garage when they moved back to West Texas. There had been a problem with the transmission since their arrival; it wouldn't move in reverse. It simply sat there like a functioning car, waiting for someone to back it out for a drive. Nonetheless, Ben opened the garage, started it up, and let it run for a few minutes each evening. Because of that, Resha knew the car would at least start and stay on. That gave her a sliver of hope.

She nodded her head. No, Ben would not leave her. Not after taking her life as he had. She would give those babies their very best day. She would pour all that was left in her chalice upon them. Nourish them. Play games that forced smiles across their lips. Make them happy. They deserved that much. She would kiss them and tell them she loved them. And then she would promise them a ride to the park. They would be delighted. She had never done that. She would load them up and start the Monte Carlo and they would sing and sing and sing themselves to sleep. And Ben would know and always know and he would never forget.

TIME AFTER

....

For the aunts and uncles;
the living and the dead

Mary was glad when the plane finally landed. She didn't think she could sit in the seat and keep her eyes open another minute. She hadn't slept at all the night before; had tossed and turned, thinking of her brother, Tenchie. Dallas to Washington wasn't an insanely long flight, but at her age, with her particular series of ailments, sitting anywhere longer than a few hours was hard on her body. By the time the plane landed, her bladder was full, and her knees ached. She was also nervous because she wasn't a frequent flyer. In fact, she hadn't experienced her first plane ride until she was in her late fifties. But her sister Bobbi Jean believed this trip was essential. And after her initial protests regarding the trip, Mary trained her thoughts on how she would endure it.

She hadn't been nervous about the flight beforehand, but as soon as the wheels of the plane bumped against the ground, her heart began to bang against her chest. She hadn't seen Bobbi Jean since they buried their older sister, Faye, the year before. Sure, they talked on the phone several times each week, but seeing Bobbi Jean in the flesh was something altogether different. She'd seen the world from LA and cruise ships while some of their family had never even left Texas.

Mary patted the tight curls of thinning hair that her beautician had spent hours perfecting the day before, placed her hand against her chest to calm herself, lifted the window cover, and exhaled so deeply that she fogged the window. "Lord, help us. This gone be a long two days," she said out loud.

She looked at the empty seat next to her and thanked God that no one had sat there. Believed that God loved her more than anyone else on the plane because the seat had remained unoccupied the entire length of the flight. The man in the seat next to the unoccupied one stood and sighed dramatically as soon as the plane came to a complete stop and the seat belt light bell dinged. He bogarted his way out to the center of the aisle, accidently elbowing the man seated in front of him in the head. He lifted his arms, right along with the other rushers around him, to gather his belongings from the overhead storage.

Mary stayed seated. She waited until they were all out. Until the plane was only occupied by the crew and other patient folks, like her, and then she begged her bones to bear with her as she gathered her things and made her way to her sister, who was supposed to be at the gate waiting for her arrival.

Bobbi Jean had been adamant about how necessary this "business" trip was. *I just don't know, Mary,* she'd said over the phone in a voice that Mary believed was a bit too uppity for her having lived the first seventeen years of her life in a two-room house with eight other people. Mary imagined her waving her hand as she spoke and batting her eyes in the way all LA women who look like Diahann Carroll must be prone to do.

We are the only three left, Mary. She sighed, and her words came out so proper and perfect that Mary swore it wasn't her sister on the other line. She imagined someone different. Someone who'd never taken a bath in a tin washtub or in used water.

They decided to meet in Washington, DC, to search for their brother—to search for Tenchie. She hadn't seen her brother in a very long time. He had been missing during Faye's funeral last year. Bobbi Jean had stayed in town longer to sort the situation out, but Mary was gone by the time he was recovered. Over the years, she'd reasoned that Tenchie was an adult—now in his early seventies—and had made the choices that led him to his current situation. Sometimes she found herself confused. Her pastor said the Bible was clear regarding what she knew about her brother. Even if Tenchie had never come out and said so, his ways were a stink to God's nostrils, a filthy thing that every Christian should flee. But sometimes, Mary wondered.

After Bobbi Jean guilted her into coming along, Mary resolved that this trip would be an opportunity for her to make things right, an opportunity for her to let God know that he had her whole heart. She would be God's own witness. She would tell her brother that he needed to repent, and he would hear the Lord's voice and be changed in an instant. And they would both be whole because, for her, everything started with Tenchie. Every act of love and every act of hate, she could trace back to him. She'd worked more than thirty years serving God, her home, and the homes of white folks. Because she served God before anyone else, she served her family and the families that hired her to his glory. She was faithful. She was faithful to them all. But she knew she'd failed Tenchie—the only one she'd failed—when she revisited the Bible without the filter of her pastor. She imagined Jesus asking her, *What do you think, Mary? If a man owns a hundred sheep, and one of them strays, will he not leave the ninety-nine and go look for the one that strayed?* She often wondered if she should've opened the door for him when he came to her in the '80s. If she had forgiven him, maybe they could've found God together.

At first, Mary had tried to get out of coming on the trip. Said, *Bobbi Jean, Tenchie don't want to be found. Tenchie love where he at.* She went on to tell her sister about her daughter's recent hysterectomy. How the girl had dealt with endometriosis and then fibroids and then just gave up and had everything removed. She'd told her about the emptiness she felt for her daughter, who pretended it didn't bother her. About how she almost didn't see her girl as a woman anymore. How the girl had earned the trouble she was having with her body.

Her older sister had cut her off. Corrected her on her name. Said, *Bobbi. Just Bobbi. I haven't been Bobbi Jean in a long time, Mary.* And then she'd commenced telling Mary about her tendency to be selfish. To only care about her children, which was such an inward way of caring. Of loving. And because Bobbi Jean was her elder by seven full years, Mary had become quiet and was now meeting her sister in Washington.

Mary's absence from her brother's life had nothing to do with God in the beginning. More than that, it was the opposite of what they'd promised each other they would always be. It was him she had been close to as a child. He was years older than she was, but they had a special connection from the day she was born until the day he left home. When she was old enough to listen, he'd tell her, *I knew you were the special one when Momma was carrying you. I sang to you in there, remember?* And she liked to pretend she did. *That's why you love me, Mae Mae*, he'd whisper, kissing her temples softly.

And the first voice she could ever remember was not her mother's or father's. It was his. It was Tenchie's, and she thought it was the sweetest thing in the world. And the sweetness she found had nothing to do with him being the only singer in the family. It was his words and all the forms of beauty he pushed from his mouth. From his lips she was Mae Mae darling, Mae Mae love, Mae Mae sugar, and Mae Mae honey. From his lips came soft blows and kisses to cuts, scrapes, and burns. He was kindness and love in the storm of their home. A balm in such a world as that.

It seemed to Mary, when she was young, that their father hated his only son and her mother would never love her in the way a mother loves her baby girl. She would always look at Mary with disappointed eyes because if she had been a boy, someone acceptable for Tenchie to play with, someone to make him right, all the crooked paths in their world would have been made straight. Their father's hate seemed to grow over the years. Mary could remember being four and hearing her father's booming voice, a voice that caused their whole house to hold its breath, beat down on her brother, who wasn't even ten, for being afraid to go to the outhouse alone. He'd punish him by locking him in and making him sleep there. He was cruel to Tenchie in ways that caused them all to drop their heads. He tried everything he could think of to draw a toughness from the boy. The days he took him to the backyard to teach him boxing were the worst, but in the end, Tenchie was tough. No one outside their house mistreated his sisters because Tenchie's punches came down on them just as hard as his father's had come down on him.

Their father didn't allow his only son to walk around singing. Singing, like fear, was for women. It was clear to them all that his biggest fear was that Tenchie would be exactly who Tenchie was. By the time Mary came along, all she knew was the tension between her parents and the strong silence in their home.

Because he wasn't allowed to sing in their father's house, Tenchie taught Mary to listen. They would spend hours at a time listening to Ray Charles, James Brown, Otis Redding, Sam Cooke, Aretha Franklin, the Isley Brothers, and so many others. Tenchie taught her to catch the words of those songs and hold them in her heart. He'd whisper the lyrics to "Try a Little Tenderness" and "You're All I Need to Get By" and together they would cry at the weight of the words. He used music to teach her about love—to teach her who she was; therefore, he understood her in ways her parents and sisters never tried to. When he stayed home and went to college locally, against his mother's advice, a part of Mary knew that he was doing it to be with her. All their sisters had left, fled the fury of their father, and Tenchie, who had the most to lose, who was the source of everything, stayed for her.

When she was seventeen, a year before she was supposed to leave home herself, her high school class went to visit the campus of her brother's school. She hadn't expected to see him. She'd expected the campus to be so sprawling that Tenchie would be as small as an ant there. But she'd grown excited when she spotted the back of a head that looked like his. She squinted her eyes to be sure that it was Tenchie. And she smiled when she was certain that she recognized the brownish tint in the small afro he was so proud of. She moved her lips to call out to him as he walked confidently across the green lawn of the campus, but then she saw the man beside him grab his hand and hold it. She watched them disappear that way, together, and she knew what she'd always known, what their father had always feared.

It took her months to confront him about what she'd seen, to ask him, *Why you can't just be right? Why you keep being like this? You'd be perfect if you was right.*

And a sadness came over his face that let her know she was asking something impossible of him, but she expected him to do what he'd always done. She expected him to choose her before himself.

Eventually, trying to pretend that he could be who their father wanted him to be got to be too much for Tenchie. Eventually, their father tried to kill him on the front lawn. Eventually, he left bloodied and in tears. Mary hated him for that.

When she finally got off the plane and pulled her carry-on out past her arrival gate, her eyes darted back and forth in search of her sister. She almost panicked when she didn't see her. When she expressed her fear of flying alone to a strange city, Bobbi Jean promised that she'd hurry from her own gate and be waiting at her sister's.

She'd said, *Oh, hush, Mary. I'll be right there. You don't have to be afraid.*

She placed her hand on her chest and said, "Sweet Jesus, help me," and tried gathering her thoughts enough to think of a plan for locating her sister. It was then that she noticed the woman standing a few feet away from her, waving both her hands and smiling widely. "Yoo-hoo," she sang, before throwing her head back laughing.

Mary's eyes widened and the fear slowly receded, but she could feel it being replaced by something else. Something that she could not quite understand. Bobbi Jean's hair, which had been a beautiful salt and pepper at Faye's funeral, was short, cropped, and honey blond. Despite the fact that they were indoors and the weather outside had looked gloomier than anything from the windows on the plane, she was wearing huge, goggle-like sunglasses and the brightest red lipstick that could possibly exist anywhere on the planet.

Mary smiled and began to pull her bag toward her.

"You almost didn't recognize me, huh?" Bobbi Jean said, smiling, almost blushing, revealing extra-white implants that looked strange but perfect against her golden skin. Mary took in her sister's full form when she opened her arms for a hug. She wore a long fur coat and Mary could see the pointy toes of her red shoes peeking from underneath it.

She let herself fall into Bobbi Jean's embrace and then pulled away to get a better look at her. She pouted and batted her eyes at her older sister. "You old silly gal. Out here looking like these young folk. Look good, though, Bobbi Jean—I mean Bobbi. You look good."

And she meant those words, but they also made her remember how she no longer looked "good" or young. They made her remember the mint-colored pantsuit she was wearing herself. They made her remember that her breasts had flattened and dropped many children ago. That her hips now carried the weight of six decades' worth of bad choices. That her backside, though still soft, was probably now dented and saggy. She couldn't be certain about that, though. She hadn't seen her backside in years.

And insecurity set in for another reason too. Bobbi Jean was educated and always used proper English—always sounded white to Mary. She had promised herself that she would try to be more proper with her English. That she would try to be more like her oldest daughter, the one she'd put through school. The one who was a professor.

"I *am* one of these young folk," Bobbi Jean said, emphasizing the words in a way that made Mary feel as if she was being mocked. "*I* told *you*, Mary, *you* stop living and *you* die. That's what happened to Lois. That's what happened to Janie Pearl. That's what happened to Faye."

Bobbi Jean was right. She was always right. She was also the only one of the siblings, besides Tenchie, another educated one, who had ever said Mary's name in the way that white people said it. The way it was meant to be said. Everyone else in her family had pronounced her name "Mae-ree."

"You must be starving, Mary. Let's get a bite to eat," Bobbi Jean said, reaching for the handle of Mary's carry-on.

Mary shook her head and said, "I got it." She let out a loud breath. "I really ain't got no appetite yet," she said, scrunching her nose as they made their way through the airport. "Maybe we can look around for Tenchie for a little bit. Maybe that'll work up something for me."

She wanted to take the lie back almost immediately. She was starving. She treated the day before plane rides in the same manner she treated days before surgery. No food, no drink, and no sleep. She'd had a cup of water and a coffee on the plane, but her stomach was otherwise empty. But she'd thought a lot about Bobbi Jean calling her selfish most of the plane ride there. She needed to show her sister that the work of God was running through her.

"You sure, Mary?" her sister replied. "We can get you settled in first. We've got all of tomorrow to look for Tenchie. You've got time to wind down from your flight."

The automatic doors of the airport opened to them and they walked out into a hard chill that caused Mary to shiver and grip the lapels of her coat.

She shook her head. There was no way she could turn back now. "The Lord say, 'Give not sleep to thine eyes, nor slumber to thine eyelids.' We find our brother and then we rest."

Bobbi Jean nodded her head and led the way to the ground transportation area.

When they were situated safely in a taxi, Bobbi Jean explained to Mary that she had been in communication with Tenchie's friend Wendell. "He gave me a list of places to look, Mary. He knows this stuff. He knows our brother." And that made Mary sad.

There were other things that Mary felt sad—felt guilty—about. Like Faye and how selfless she had been when Tenchie fell ill five years ago. Faye hadn't been the sanctified one. She had been the drunk most of her life, but she was the one who did the Christian thing and flew out to DC, packed their brother's life up, and moved him to Lubbock with her. She was the one who took him in. By that time, Mary had raised all her children and only had herself to take care of. She should've have spoken up and volunteered. Instead, she had remained silent and let Faye take on the weight of their brother.

And Tenchie was angry through most of it. Through the therapy, through finding out that he would not return to his former self, and through learning that there were parts of his brain that would never recover. He cursed Faye about keeping him away from his practice, from his money, and from Wendell.

Tenchie was a smart man. A genius almost, and Bobbi Jean liked to say that's why West Texas couldn't hold him. While he was there with Faye, where he had been reared and brought up, he walked to the library each morning and read whatever he could get his hands on. People in the neighborhood took to calling him Rain Man, but he didn't care. He wanted to find himself again and leave and stay gone as he had originally intended.

Faye worried about him. Called the remaining sisters, Mary in Dallas and Bobbi Jean in Los Angeles, begging them to give him some type of temporary relief from the place, but they always responded that they were too busy. They all left her hanging until she could hang no more, and when she gave up the ghost and passed on, they both agreed to let him go back to the home he longed for. Bobbi Jean, the oldest living sibling, put herself in charge of his disability and took his word that he had a friend—had a place to live—and just let him go.

The hotel they checked into was nice. After she relieved her bladder, Mary wanted badly to fall onto one of the crisp, plush beds in the room, but it had been her suggestion that they drop their bags off and visit the first cluster of shelters on Wendell's list. Bobbi Jean suggested they catch a cab to the first spot and walk to the others from there.

"I'm a West Coaster, Mary. I'm not built to walk around in such cold," she said, finally removing the sunglasses from her face.

And after the third try—after their third *No Tenchie Hobbs on our list*—she was ready to give in to her hunger and maybe even tell Bobbi Jean it was time for them to rest. After all, she had proved her dedication to the cause and to God. She had presented her worn body as a living sacrifice, and now it was time to care for it.

Right when she was ready to open her mouth and let her words spring forth, Bobbi Jean said, "I know you want to keep going, Mary, but I've got to get something in my stomach. I still have meds I need to get in me."

Mary silently thanked God for her sister's rheumatoid arthritis and hypertension. She shrugged her shoulders and said, "Okay, Bobbi. Let's get something. I don't want you sick."

And the two of them eyed their surroundings. After two taxis and a three-block walk, they were far enough from their hotel to decide to eat somewhere close. However, they didn't know where they were or what was around.

Bobbi Jean pulled out her phone and Mary moved in close to her in an attempt to warm herself and see the screen. They stood there, kind of huddling, almost embracing, as Bobbi Jean fidgeted with her phone.

"I know," Bobbi Jean said, looking up at Mary. "Let's just ask someone what's good. I, for one, would rather have a recommendation from a human." She dropped her phone back into her purse.

Bobbi Jean said, "Excuse me," to a passing stranger and the lady, a plump white woman with a mannish look, stopped and listened to her sister attentively.

"I know a place you girls will love," the woman said to Bobbi Jean. "All kinds of food. Good atmosphere. It's a safe place," she said with a wink.

She gave Bobbi Jean the address and pointed them in the direction a few blocks away.

Bobbi Jean thanked her and they made their way toward the sunset to where they would finally eat.

The restaurant wasn't an upscale one. In fact, it looked more like a bar from the outside. Mary couldn't help but wonder if they were in the wrong place.

"You sure this it?" she asked her sister, who was smiling wide as she looked up at the neon marquee.

"She said the place was called Sophie's. This is it," she said.

Mary shrugged her shoulders. At this point, Mary was so hungry she didn't care where they ate.

When they stepped into the place, her eyes darted around wildly. The person at the hostess podium had a thin mustache, but Mary could not determine what gender they were. Neon condoms decorated the floor of the place. To Mary, none of the people were who she thought they should be. She could not tell the men from the women and she felt that the confusion was on purpose. From the podium, Mary could see a jukebox next to the bar, and what looked like a man dressed in leather leaned against it while what looked like a man in a dress leaned into him.

Bobbi Jean began to laugh and shake her head. The person behind the podium smiled, considered Bobbi Jean for a moment, and shifted her gaze to Mary.

"How many in your party, lover?" the person asked.

"Oh. I—I don't know if we staying," Mary said, looking at Bobbi Jean, who held up an index finger that was meant as a request to be allowed to finish laughing.

"Of course we're staying, Mary," she said, as her laughter begin to fade away. "I'm just tickled that the woman who sent us in here thought we were a couple," she said to the person behind the podium. "You see, we're sisters," she said, waving her finger between herself and Mary. "She's my little sister, not my lover," Bobbi Jean said before going into another fit of laughter.

Mary kept quiet and moved in closer to her sister. She did not want the spirits in the place to attach themselves to her.

She didn't say anything when they were first seated in the dimness of the booth. She looked down at the vintage plastic-covered floral seats and thought about their mother's house. Not the two-room shotgun one from when they were children, but the one she'd bought after they were all grown. The one Bobbi Jean never visited.

Her sister ordered the Cobb salad without bacon and Mary wanted to smack her lips when she said the no bacon part. They had been raised on hogs, every part of them. Bobbi Jean and that Seventh Day stuff said bacon was a bad thing. She also ordered wine, which made Mary want to pray for her. She was such a lost thing.

When the waiter delivered the meal, Mary wanted to hesitate with her taco salad, wanted to show God that the hands that prepared the food mattered to her, but the fajita steak and the tomatoes and the cheese and the beans all looked so perfect that she dug in right after saying a quick grace.

"I know you didn't want to eat here, Mary," her sister said, as she mixed her salad together.

Mary let her eyes shift from her own salad to her sister and she noted the crow's feet around her sister's wide eyes.

"I'm all right," Mary replied in a quiet voice.

"But you didn't want to eat here," Bobbi Jean said again.

Mary dropped her fork and looked around the room. She turned her eyes back to her sister, who was now staring at her seriously. "God ain't pleased with this kind of mess," Mary said, stabbing her index finger into the table.

Bobbi Jean dropped her fork and sighed. "How much of your life do you spend doing that, Mary? Judging? Being mad? Unhappy?"

Mary gently slammed her fist against the table. "The Lord put us here to judge sin. Read your word," she said, nodding her head at her sister.

Bobbi Jean let out another deep sigh. "You used to have a life—a smile. You were just the prettiest thing. Remember that?" she asked. "People loved you. Wanted to be around you. I don't know if it was that—that man—that Lee, or the lousy one you married and stayed with all those years," she said, flipping her hand, like something dirty and unwanted. "Constantly putting their hands on you. But you lost yourself somewhere. You are misery, child. Misery."

Mary gasped and clutched her heart with her hand. She wanted to tell her sister that she had no right to speak about her life in that way. She wanted to tell her that she was holy and no man had power over her, but she was tired of telling people that—telling her children that—telling her ex-husband that. "The Lord keep me just fine. This ain't about me, Bobbi Jean. I—"

"Our brother stayed away because he couldn't tell us he was gay. He couldn't even say it because that would've made it real and he wanted us to be safe from it," Bobbi Jean said, leaning into the table. "And the sad part is that he was always the beautiful one. The cleanest thing we had in our lives." She was stabbing her index finger into the table to enunciate the end of each word and Mary could see the small speckles of spit spraying from her mouth. "We left him out there, Mary Glen. And now we're searching for him like he's some vagabond. He should've always had a home in us," she said weakly.

Mary jumped at hearing her middle name pass through her sister's lips. Bobbi Jean hadn't said it in so long, not since she moved away and became her fancy self. She had given up on all their middle names. Declared them a country thing and given up on them. But Mary also jumped because Tenchie had known that she knew and she'd told him that because he was himself, he could never have a home in her.

"And it was always you he loved the most," Bobbi Jean said quietly. "Wouldn't God just want you to love him too?"

Mary looked down at the table. She didn't want her sister to see the guilt in her eyes. Tenchie *had* been good to her. Even though she refused to speak to him after he left—after he refused to be right and stay with her. He had been the one to send her the monthly checks when she was alone with two children. He had seen her through that until she found a husband and married. He was really the only support system she had in those days, as all her other siblings were busy with their own lives and families and her mother was struggling to find her way through their father's death.

She often thought about that year in the '80s—that year he flew out to Texas after their father died. The time he told her to find something—to find the Lord. She was living in a trailer on a bit of land with the father of her first two children. Lee liked to slap her around on Friday nights, so when she flung the trailer door open and found Tenchie standing there one Saturday morning, she was too shocked and surprised to remember to hide her black eye.

She would never forget how wide Tenchie's eyes got. How he reached out and tried to stroke her cheek and how she pulled away as if she thought he'd hurt her. How he looked hurt and cursed and said, *Shit, Mae Mae. Why didn't you call me?*

She didn't let him into the trailer. She stepped outside and said, *You can't come in here. Ain't welcome here.*

And he looked sad and hurt and swallowed it all. *I understand*, he said. *I understand, Mae Mae love.*

Even though he didn't ask, she stood before him with her arms crossed and tried to explain why she couldn't let him. *I—I just wanted you, Tenchie. You was everything to me*, she said. *But you wouldn't hear me, so now you . . .* She let her words trail off.

His eyes dropped to the ground and he cleared his throat. *I uh*, he started and then shrugged his shoulders and adjusted them high so that he looked strong and proud standing before her.

After a while he looked at her and said, *You worshipping the wrong god, Mae Mae darling. But I tell you what. I'm about to find him and whup his ass in a way that'll show you he's a man. After that, you go find a real god to serve.*

And then he walked away.

Mary wasn't surprised when Lee came to the trailer later that night, bloodied and eyes swollen so shut that she couldn't see the whites of them. He gathered his belongings, called her family crazy, and left her life for good. From then until she married a few years later, Tenchie made sure she and the children always had a home with a refrigerator full of food. He was good about his weekly calls and making sure there was enough money in his packages to cover them through birthdays and Christmases. Even though she wouldn't talk to him, he was consistent in all he did for her.

Tenchie started calling on Thursday nights after that visit. He must've got her number from their mother or one of the sisters or something, but he dialed it every Thursday, like clockwork. Those first few times, right after the visit, he just repeated hello over and over until Mary hung up. Around the third or fourth time he called, he simply put the phone to some type of music player and let a song she'd never heard play. She cried that first time he played what she later learned was Cyndi Lauper's "Time After Time." The words were beautiful, and she knew he wanted her to hold them in her heart. And she cried to that song every Thursday night for two years, never hanging up before the repetition of the chorus right at the end. That was the part where she could always catch him whispering as the music faded out, *Time after time.* She missed those whispers when the calls finally stopped, and she felt like he'd left her all over again.

. . .

Mary opened her mouth carefully. She wanted to make Bobbi Jean understand what she herself couldn't. "I—I—"

"It's almost my time, Mary Glen," Bobbi Jean cut her off. "I'll be seventy-five in three months. I got to do right. I don't have children to carry my legacy. Not like you, I don't. I just want to live. I don't want . . ." She let her words trail off, and Mary was sad for her.

"That curse ain't real, Bobbi. The devil is a lie," she said. "It's all coincidental. Whoever heard of everyone dying in the order of they birth at seventy-five? They deaths ain't got nothing to do with—"

A smile broke out on her sister's face. "Girl, I just want to dance," Bobbi Jean said, cutting her off in a singsong voice. "And sing in a voice that could melt the moon," she added, sliding from the booth slowly, almost as if she weren't her age.

Mary watched Bobbi Jean make her way to the jukebox and gently ask the men leaning against it if she could get to it. Mary thought about how young her sister looked standing there in her high-waisted Levi's and the short-cut long-sleeved T-shirt. She couldn't imagine walking around in the heeled booties her sister wore, but she couldn't help remembering that there was a time when she had. Bobbi Jean's words rang in her ear: You *stop living and* you *die*.

She could feel the weak smile spread across her own lips when she heard the first line of the song. *Lying in my bed, I hear the clock tick*. She tapped her fingers on the table and closed her eyes, remembering the words to the song. She felt herself smiling, and by the time she slid from the booth, the only thing she felt was what was stirring in her stomach. It was the same thing she felt on Sundays when she shouted all over the church. When she spoke in tongues and leapt for joy. The stirring in her stomach was that and she knew to answer its call.

She made her way over to the jukebox, where Bobbi Jean stood with her eyes closed, and she let the music move inside her, raising her hands above her head and moving her hips to the beat. She closed her eyes and cradled her waist with her hands. She let them crawl up her body slowly, as if she were exploring herself for the first time. She remembered being a girl, being free, and she became herself again. She wanted to stay in the moment. To remain free. And then she thought of David and God and Jesus. She told herself, *God is here.*

She felt she'd danced for hours when she finally opened her eyes. She scanned the room for Bobbi Jean, who was leaning against the jukebox, smiling, and what appeared to be a man dressed as a woman hovered over her in conversation. When she saw that Mary was looking at her, she tipped the beer bottle she was holding and nodded her head in her direction. That's when Mary looked down at herself. That's when she saw that her shirt was gone.

She stopped dancing and tried cover her bra with one arm, as she looked around the floor for her shirt and made her way back to the booth. She spotted the mint-colored blouse next to the booth they had eaten in, put it on right there, buttoned it up crooked, bundled up in her coat, and walked out of the bar.

She was crying when Bobbi Jean walked out the door just a

moment after her, when her big sister embraced her and whispered, *There, there.* When the cries became soft, Bobbi Jean held her at arm's length, looked in her eyes, and said, "Dancing is the voice of God, Mary. Don't ever be ashamed for dancing."

Mary nodded her head without speaking and thought about telling her sister how good her body felt, how right the dancing had made her feel, but she couldn't help thinking of her brother, somewhere alone in the coldness of the strange city.

"They said we should look a few blocks over. Said there's a tent city that hasn't been broken up yet. We do that and we turn in, okay?" Bobbi Jean said, as if she'd read her mind.

Mary nodded and followed her sister. They were quiet as they navigated the noisy streets, and she appreciated that. So many things were running through her mind. She wanted to get somewhere and open her Bible. She wanted to get somewhere and pray. She wanted to ground herself in what had kept her. These feelings were not what she was expecting. She wanted to do the work of God. She had no idea what was happening inside her.

And she was thinking of these things when they passed the alleyway where she saw him, when she knew him despite the oversized hooded coat wrapped tight around him, when she recognized his dirty face and the gait Bobbi Jean said he'd developed after the stroke, when she spotted him empty-eyed and slack-jawed, walking in her direction. And for a moment, Mary couldn't move. She hadn't seen him since he was a young man, and even as an old one, he was everything she remembered.

"Bobbi," she called out to her sister, who was, by then, several feet ahead of her. But she couldn't open her mouth to speak more words, so her sister's eyes followed her gaze.

"Tenchie," her sister called out in a scream that was almost a cry. "Brother," she said, opening her arms. "My brother, come here."

Mary thought he would turn and walk away. He looked down at himself and then back up at them before letting his shoulders drop even more. He walked over to them slowly, and, instead of falling into Bobbi Jean's open arms, he fell toward Mary, and she quickly moved to open herself up.

And for years after that night, years after Bobbi Jean's death that next year, years after Tenchie's the year after that, she wondered what they looked like to people passing by, him weeping into her shoulder, her holding him and swaying as if they were dancing while she whispered the lyrics to that Cyndi Lauper song in his ear, like a prayer to God, hoping it would save them.

ACKNOWLEDGMENTS

YHWH: All the glory and all the thanks.

When you spend years writing a book, the number of folks who offer meaningful insight and direction grows long and wide. Words of thanks will never be enough.

Samantha Shea: Thank you for all the support, editorial and otherwise. Even before you became my agent, I knew you were the best for me.

Phoebe Robinson: Thank you for being the powerhouse who created an imprint where being seen and heard are commonplace. Your support in this work has made all the difference. You are appreciated.

My editor, Pilar Garcia-Brown: For believing in and loving this work, for helping to make it better, thank you.

Amber Oliver: Thank you for seeing *Holler, Child* for what it was from the start and for your continued support.

To the team at Tiny Reparations Books, especially Sarah, Jamie, and Emi: All the gratitude for the hard work and the love. And long live the cover artists.

To the programs and institutions whose funding, space, and community made this work possible—Kimbilio, MacDowell, Yaddo, Hedgebrook, Art Omi, The Camargo Foundation, *A Public Space*, and the Bread Loaf Writers' Conference: I will always be grateful. Always.

To the teachers, writers, readers, and friends whose feedback and encouragement helped shape these stories: Y'all are holy.

To those of you so ready and willing to indulge me daily via texts, phone conversations, or in person (my everydays): Thanks for holding me down on the regular. Love y'all big big.

To anyone who has contributed to this work in any way: My gratitude forever.

ABOUT THE AUTHOR

....

LaToya Watkins's debut novel, *Perish*, was published to great acclaim in 2022. Her writing has appeared in *A Public Space*, *The Sun* magazine, *McSweeney's*, and *The Kenyon Review*, among other publications. She has received grants, scholarships, and fellowships from Kimbilio, The Camargo Foundation, MacDowell, Yaddo, and elsewhere. She lives and teaches in a suburb of Dallas.